Messages Found in an Oxygen Bottle

Bob Shaw

THE NESFA PRESS
BOX G, MIT BRANCH P.O.
CAMBRIDGE, MA 02139-0910
1986

FIRST EDITION

LIBRARY OF CONGRESS CATALOG NO. 86-061272

INTERNATIONAL STANDARD BOOK NO.
0-915368-33-1 (REGULAR EDITION)
0-915368-88-9 (SLIPCASED EDITION)

Copyright Acknowledgments

"Introduction," copyright © 1986 by Bob Shaw.

"The Bermondsey Triangle Mystery," copyright © 1977 by Bob Shaw. Speech given at Eastercon (1977) and first printed in *Maya* 14, ed. by Rob Jackson.

"Pyrotechnics," copyright © 1954 by Bob Shaw. First appeared in *Hyphen* 12, ed. by Walter Willis.

"Ad Astra?" copyright © 1986 by Bob Shaw. First appeared in *Vector*.

"The Man in the Grey Flannel Toga," copyright © 1960 by Bob Shaw. First appeared in *Hyphen* 24, ed. by Walter Willis.

"Ten Years, But Not Decayed," copyright © 1984 by Bob Shaw. Speech given at Seacon 84/ Eurocon and first printed in *Serious Science*.

"BoSh Goes Loco," copyright © 1955 by Bob Shaw. First appeared in *Hyphen* 14, ed. by Walter Willis.

"The Return of the Backyard Spaceship," copyright © 1976 by Bob Shaw. Speech given at Mancon and first printed in *Maya* 11, ed. by Rob Jackson.

"More Canadian Capers," copyright © 1958 by Bob Shaw. First appeared as "Canadian Capers(2)" in *Hyphen* 21, ed. by Walter Willis.

"Up the Conjunction," copyright © 1978 by Bob Shaw. Speech given at Skycon and first printed in *Drilkjis* 3.

Dust jacket painting ©1986 by Bob Eggleton

INTRODUCTION

Did you ever try to explain to a non-SF person exactly what a convention is?

You can't do it! Not properly, anyway. No matter how much explanation and detail you go into about the various events and activities, you're always left with the sense of having failed to make your audience understand that unique quality which makes the whole greater than the sum of its parts, which makes a convention something special to *you*.

There is a similar problem with SF fanzine writing.

A newcomer to the fanzine field usually expects solid blocks of SF criticism, comment and news; and quite often he recoils the age-old cry, "There's too much irrelevant and personal material in fanzines, and not enough about what brought us all together in the first place."

But if he* perserveres with fanzines he will discover that

------

* Please note that I stick to the old grammatical rule that in order to avoid unwieldy sentence constructions the masculine pronoun stands for both genders.

much fanzine writing, as with conventions, has that special Ingredient X which is so hard to define. The word we coined for it long ago was "fannishness."

It is possible to attend a fan meeting where the subject of SF doesn't crop up at all in an entire evening's conversation, and yet to leave that meeting with the pleasantly sated feeling which might come if nothing *but* SF had been discussed. The reason for this phenomenon is that everything said has been filtered through science-fictional minds. In other words — the conversation had fannishness.

Well, the pieces you'll find in this book also have fannishness.

They were written as labours of love, without thought of material reward, for the sheer joy of their inherent fannishness.

Fannishness! the word keeps appearing because it's the only one we have for a rare and precious commodity — and if you don't already understand it I can only suggest that you read on . . .

CONTENTS

This book was designed by Jim Mann; set in Times Roman by Jim Mann and Andy Cowan at Typo-Tech Reproduction Center, Inc. of Cambridge, MA, with assistance from George Flynn, Pam Fremon, Susan Hammond, and a horde of others; and printed on Neutral pH 60# paper by Braun-Brumfield, Inc. of Ann Arbor, Michigan.

MESSAGES FOUND IN AN OXYGEN BOTTLE

THE BERMONDSEY
TRIANGLE MYSTERY

Pardon me if I don't seem my usual robust self today. I went round a few room parties last night, living it up — now I'm trying to live it down. Actually, the night started to go a bit wrong when I found myself at a *temperance* room party, which wasn't quite what I had planned on. I'm not saying the host was unfannish — but that was the first convention party I'd ever been to where I was expected to buy Tupperware.

I got out of there in a hurry, because we've got all the Tupperware we need at home. Our fridge, the pantry, all the cupboards, are filled with Tupperware. There's no room for food — just these heaps and heaps of plastic boxes which break your nails when you try to open the lids. When I die I'm going to be put away in a Tupperware coffin — I think I ordered it last night — and the worms just won't be able to get near me. When alien super-beings land on the deserted Earth in a few thousand years from now and start looking around for a human being to resurrect, I'll probably be fresh as a daisy in there. The only trouble is, the alien super-beings probably won't be able to get my lid off...

Anyway, by the time I got to a proper room-party I hadn't

had a drink for about half an hour, and you know how it is with booze — a long period of abstinence like that really whets your appetite for it. I think I may possibly have imbibed a little too much, because this morning I had a bad headache, and there was no Alka-Seltzer or aspirin. Luckily, one of the committee was kind enough to nip out and get me some pain-killer they make in a little shop just around the corner from here — it's a local anaesthetic — and that enabled me to come here as planned to tell you all about the Bermondsey Triangle mystery.

Now, to me, one of the most intriguing and *sinister* things about the Bermondsey Triangle mystery is that nobody has ever heard of it!

I mean, practically everybody has heard about the old Bermuda Triangle mystery, and it's even got to the point of popularity where the mystery is self-perpetuating. Did you know that the last three ships to disappear in the Bermuda Triangle were carrying cargoes of books about the Bermuda Triangle mystery? There's so much demand for them in that area that whole fleets loaded up with the books are charging about all over the Caribbean, running into each other, getting sunk, and adding to the legend. They're littered about all over the seabed, and what worries me is that pulp paper is terribly absorbent. One of these days we're going to hear a loud slurping noise — and the Caribbean will disappear! And Castro will blame it on the CIA ...

There's even a new TV series about the Bermuda Triangle — called *The Fantastic Journey* — which combines the scientific authenticity of *Space: 1999* with the gripping story quality of *Look at Life* on a visit to Bootle. I mustn't start being sarcastic about *Space: 1999* again, though — last time I did that I offended the show's regular viewers, and they both wrote to me about it. And I think one of them had even gone to the expense of buying a new crayon! Mention of *The Fantastic Journey* reminds me that one of my problems with the show is that, after all those *Planet of the Apes* programmes, I can't bear to look directly at Roddy McDowell any more. All I see is Galen ... *skinned!* It's hard to think of anything more revolting.

But I was talking about the self-perpetuating nature of the Bermuda Triangle mystery, a process which I find interesting. A vaguely parallel case has occurred up in the Lake District, where I live. There's a local confectionery called Kendal mint cake which, for some reason, is always brought along by climbers who are tackling Everest. The manufacturers set great store by this, and on the waxy wrappers always list the numerous mountaineering expeditions of the last fifty years which sustained themselves on difficult climbs by eating Kendal mint cake. What they carefully *don't* mention is the fate of the Peruvian Everest expedition of 1949, which was swept away on the south face, not by snow ... but by an avalanche of discarded Kendal mint cake wrappers.

This shows the dangers of being a litter lout. It really is antisocial to go around throwing down old bus tickets and chocolate wrappers— except, of course, on the Continent, where they have a much better class of litter. One of the things that appealed to my snob instinct on my first trip across the Channel— it was on a day trip to Calais— was that even the *garbage* was in French.

Bst this is getting away from the Bermondsey Triangle mystery, which is my main subject today. "What *is* the Bermondsey Triangle mystery?" you must be asking yourselves. If you aren't, I've been wasting my time up here throwing out these tantalising hints, planting fish-hooks. That's something that authors do, you know. They go around planting fish-hooks. Other people plant seeds; authors plant fish-hooks. It's really stupid — because nothing ever grows from fish-hooks. I think the worms come along and eat them. Especially if they're worms like the ones I've got in my garden. The soil in my garden is so poor that the worms go around in gangs attacking birds. One of them savaged the postman last week!

I know, I know! This is getting away from the subject of the Bermondsey Triangle mystery, as well. In fact, some of you are saying I can't get away from the subject of the Bermondsey Triangle mystery when I haven't even got near it. Some of you may even be entertaining doubts that there *is* a Bermondsey Triangle mystery.

Well, let me tell you... There's another funny thing — that business about entertaining doubts. Why do we always *entertain* doubts, while the best that can happen to more deserving cases such as beliefs and convictions is that they'll be firmly held? It hardly seems fair.

Now... what was I talking about? Oh, yes — the Bermondsey Triangle mystery. This first came to my attention about twenty years ago, and I want to emphasize that I'm talking about direct, first-hand experience here — unlike these literary charlatans who write sensational books based on old newspaper clippings which were probably all wrong to start off with.

My first tiny and apparently insignificant clue was... You know, I *love* the way all tales of scientific discovery start off with a tiny and apparently insignificant clue — though I suppose it has to be that way. When James Watt was getting ready to invent the steam engine the only thing he had to inspire him was the bobbing up and down of the lid of a hot kettle, and his genius lay in seeing its potential. I mean, if he had been watching the kettle boil and suddenly it had gone *toot-toot* and shot off in the direction of London, picking up passengers and collecting mailbags, *anybody* could have got the idea of the steam locomotive from it. Though James Watt, being a true genius, might have jumped up and said, "If only we could harness this energy to make tea!"

(Come to think of it, perhaps that's what actually happens — the tea I get on British Rail tastes like it came out of the engine, though only a tea connoisseur like Ethel Lindsay could be absolutely certain. In view of that fact, I feel no guilt about telling you the method I have devised for getting free tea on train journeys. They operate a two-man system when they're bringing the tea around — the first bloke comes along asking who wants tea, and if anybody does he takes his money and gives him a plastic cup, which acts both as a tea container and a receipt. A few minutes later the second bloke works his way along the train, filling all the cups. So all you have to do, before leaving home, is to make sure you pack a few plastic cups, and set one out in front of you at the appropriate moment...)

But all this is straying away from the subject of the Bermondsey Triangle mystery. I don't know why it keeps happening — must be something I wrote. This tiny and apparently insignificant clue I started to tell you about was a strange aberration in the otherwise fairly unremarkable behaviour of James White. Jim, of course, is a writer whose name is well-known to all readers of journals such as *Analog, New Worlds,* and *Stubb's Gazette.*

He is also, as everybody knows, a very steady, respectable, and sober person — compared to many other science fiction writers, that is. Admittedly, he has done a few odd things in his life. There was that time when he worked for a tailoring concern, and an encyclopaedia salesman called at his home one evening... Jim brought him in and sold him a suit!

But occasional lapses like that apart, he lives a very even sort of life — which is why my curiosity was aroused when Jim abruptly disappeared for four days. I remember the occasion very well, because it happened one Easter — a time when you would expect a man like him to be at home with his wife and family, helping the children roll eggs down hillsides, and spoiling the whole thing for them by lecturing them about the mechanics of inclined planes, and about how it was all just another way of demonstrating Newton's ideas about inertia and gravitation. All authors who have sold to *Analog* tend to go on like that.

Unlike a ship or a plane which disappears in the Bermuda Triangle, however, Jim reappeared in his old haunts a few days later — but he was a changed man! He was tired and shaken, his eyes were glazed over, there was a strange spirituous smell from his breath, and he was incoherent about what had happened to him. He had obviously been through some traumatic, mind-warping experience which was too awful to talk about, perhaps too awful to comprehend.

I have to admit that I didn't investigate the matter fully at that time, because I was busy with other important scientific researches — namely work on my perpetual motion machine. I slaved away over that machine for many years before reluctantly giving up. In the end I was forced to admit that — no matter what ingenious mechanisms I invented, no matter what clever refinements I tried — there was just no way to stop the blasted thing. This was a big disappointment to me, but at least it gave me more time to study Jim White's behaviour, which had steadily grown more mysterious and intriguing.

He kept vanishing every Easter — always returning in the same comatose condition — and then, to my horror, it began to happen in November as well! His condition was obviously deteriorating. I began following him on these strange excursions, regardless of any physical danger involved — us dedicated researchers are like that, you see — and found that the same thing was happening to hundreds of other apparently normal men and women. Twice a year they were drawn, lemming-like, to some mysteriously prearranged point, where they milled around for several days — often having no rest throughout the entire period — before disbanding and returning to their normal lives.

What, I wondered, was it all about? What occult power was influencing them to make them behave in this fashion?

Well, the first thing a scientist does when investigating a widespread phenomenon like this is to organise the data and impose some kind of order on it. Actually, that's not quite true. The very first thing a scientist does in a case like this is to apply for a Government grant, to keep him in beer and smokes during his labours, but I knew I wouldn't get any money from the Establishment. There had been ill will between me and the authorities ever since I reported a smuggling gang, run by a chap named Leacock, to the Customs and Excise and they had failed to do anything about it. It turned out that this gang were being fiendishly clever — they only smuggled stuff there was no duty on! The authorities are powerless against men like that . . . so naturally they resented me for exposing their incompetence. They covered up their embarrassment by threatening to prosecute *me* for wasting their time, so I knew there was no point in applying for Government money.

Instead I drew a map of the country and plotted out all the locations where I knew the strange mass hysteria had occurred. And it came out like this: (See Diagram A on the top of the next page.)

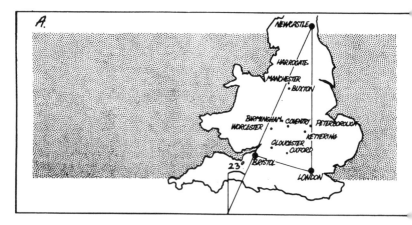

Note the significant shape of the plot! A triangle! Can this be a coincidence? I ask you, CAN THIS BE A COINCIDENCE? Of course not!

Because this is just a rough diagram I can't show the precise trigonometries I calculated, but suffice to say that the bottom right-hand corner of the triangle is positioned in the London borough of Bermondsey — hence the name I have given to the entire area involved. (In actual fact, the corner of the triangle proved to be located a little further south... To be totally precise, it is in the back room of a Chinese take-away in Peckham High Street... but who in his right mind would want to hear a talk about the Peckham Triangle mystery?)

Now, as soon as I got an inkling of what I might be on to, I realised I needed expert help in unravelling the mystery involved, and I began looking around for somebody with the necessary intellectual qualities. My first choice was L. Ron Hubbard, but I had lost touch with him soon after he invented Scientology and... I have to be careful about how

I say this ... made a cult of himself. I then contacted a friend who shall be nameless, because he is on the Seacon '79 committee. He had the right sort of mental attributes, but he was too busy getting Brighton ready for its first convention. In fact, when he heard I would be addressing this convention he asked me to pass on a message to all of you who have asked questions about Brighton in general, and in particular about the famous Brighton peer.

Talking about the Brighton peer, he said, "This criminal lunatic, who operates from the rooftops of tall buildings in central Brighton — thus forcing people to carry umbrellas at all times of the year — has not been apprehended at the time of writing, but the local police are confident he will be behind bars by 1979. There is some doubt about which bars he will actually be behind, but a close watch is being kept on all licensed premises in the area. A new clue about his identity has come from a tip-off that he is an East German who defected over the Berlin Wall. 'That is a superhuman feat, considering the height of the wall,' said a spokesman for the Brighton police, 'and shows the calibre of the man we're up against.'"

That's getting away from the subject of the Bermondsey Triangle again, but I thought you deserved the break — after all, none of you has done me any harm. I was saying that I was at a loss about who to turn to for help in sorting out this mystery, then I thought of the perfect man for the job ... that great German-Irish writer, scholar, and scientific researcher — Von Donegan!

I had trouble finding Von Donegan, because he moves around a lot — with the sort of books he writes he finds it advisable. I tried his various clubs — the Playboy Club, Foyle's Book Club, the Shillelagh (that's an Irish club) — but he wasn't at any of those places. I was getting desperate when I remembered reading that you have only to stand in Piccadilly Circus long enough and you will eventually meet everybody in the world. This seemed a good logical approach, so I went and stood there and, sure enough, I did meet people from all parts of the globe, and some from the One Tun as well.

Piccadilly Circus really lived up to its reputation, because one of the first people I met was a genuine Bolivian Indian! He told me he was in England to research a science fiction novel he was writing about Ian Watson. Then I was approached and propositioned by a lady of the town, but when she noticed my BSFA badge she made an excuse and left. I have often since wondered what she thought BSFA meant. She possibly figured out that the BS stood for Bob Shaw, but the mind boggles at what she might have made of the rest. The next person to come along was Ian Watson, who told me he was a bit worried by a new delusion he had about being followed everywhere by a Bolivian Indian...

And finally, just as the immutable laws of probability said he would, along came Von Donegan. To those of you who don't understand the mathematics of chance this might seem an unlikely coincidence, but probability math is a wonderful thing. For instance, if two people lose each other in a large department store the laws of probability say there's no guarantee they'll *ever* meet up again *unless one of them stands still.* When you think of it, this is not a very helpful statement. In fact, it makes the poor lost person's dilemma even worse — because now he doesn't even know if he should start searching around or just stand there. And if you stand around too long some sales assistant will come along and start undressing you. This could be quite good fun, except that they always start by detaching your arms and head.

Anyway, I was talking about my meeting with Von

Donegan. Strangely enough, he didn't seem all that pleased to see me. He was hurrying past with a furtive expression on his face when I stepped out of a shop doorway and grabbed him by the lapels of his raincoat. He stared at me ... and we danced for a while ... then he said, "Are you following me?"

"Certainly not," I said.

"Thank God for that," he said. "I must be losing my mind—I keep thinking I'm being followed by another science fiction writer and a bloody Red Indian."

"Bolivian," I said.

"No, it's true," he said.

I took him into a nearby pub to steady his nerves and ordered two large gin-and-tonics. He grabbed both bottles of tonic and poured them into his own gin.

"What are you doing?" I said.

"Diluting my gin," he replied. "I always use two bottles because I'm part German—this is typical two-tonic efficiency."

"That's a good one," I said, trying to humour him. "What squirts out of a siphon into your whisky glass and makes sarcastic remarks?"

"I don't know," he said.

"Caustic soda," I said. "Do you get it? Caustic soda!"

"My God," he said nervously, "and I thought *I* was going mad—I knew I should never have ventured inside the Bermondsey Triangle."

"That's what I wanted to talk to you about," I said, seizing the opportunity. I ordered two more gins, and three tonics, and over the next hour or so got the scientific explanation for the Bermondsey Triangle mystery out of him.

The story goes back some two million years, or it might be ten million years—Von Donegan didn't want to be pinned down too much on precise dates—and it turned out that my

Bermondsey Triangle was, in fact, the cradle of civilisation on Earth. Forget all that stuff about Lake Victoria and Lake Rudolph and Mesopotamia and the Valley of the Nile — this is where it all happened. Right here!

And not only did the human race start off here, but the area was inhabited by no less than four non-human civilisations, as well! There's one thing you can say for Von Donegan — he certainly gives value for money.

This diagram (Diagram B) shows the British Isles as they were two million or ten million years ago. There was Ireland on the west, looking pretty much the way it looks today. Then there was the high ground of Scotland and Wales close by. The reason they are so close is something to do with the science of plate tectonics. At one time — it sounds ridiculous, I know — all the continents were whizzing about all over the place on plates!

And at one stage, America and Canada came shooting across the Atlantic and crashed into Ireland — which must have played hell with their no-claims bonus. As well as

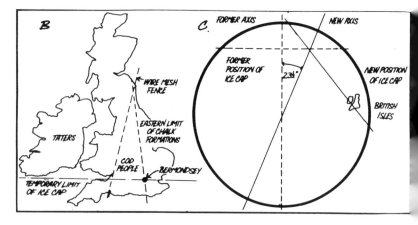

pushing Ireland closer to England, that same collision formed the mountains of Wales, the Lake District, and the Scottish Highlands — that's what I call typical tectonic efficiency. America and Canada, having done all that damage, then sneaked back to where they had come from, without even leaving a note with their names and addresses.

At the time I'm speaking of, the whole east and lower side of England was covered by a shallow sea, the waters of which were warm and clear — and which provided an ideal breeding ground for a very large and intelligent species of cod. The civilisation of the Cod People flourished apace for many centuries. They were a happy, contented sort of race, whose only vice was that they liked to get a bit high every Saturday night on their native drink, which was known as codswallop.

The only thorn in their sides was that a short distance to the west, in the fertile plains of prehistoric Ireland and Wales, another intelligent race had sprung up. They had quite literally sprung up, because this was a species of giant tubers, known as Taters. I have spoken on a previous occasion about the ability of vegetables to develop intelligence, and this new research vindicates everything I said. The civilisation of the Taters flourished apace for many centuries, as well ... (This is just like a bit from *Last and First Men,* isn't it? Olaf Stapledon, move over!) ... and their culture reached some degree of sophistication, with a well-developed caste system. The evidence indicates that the ruling caste of aristocrats were known as King Edwards, and there is even a legend that a young, high-born female Tater dashed up to her mother one day, her eyes shining ... all of them ... and said, "Mum, I'm engaged!"

Her mother said, "Who to? Remember you're a King Edward, and you can't just marry anybody who comes along."

And the girl Tater said, "It's Dickie Davies, of 'The World of Sport'."

And her mother said, "You can't marry that common-tater!"

Anyway, sad to relate, enmity developed between the Cod People and the Taters. It was mainly on account of the Cod People's noisy booze-ups every Saturday night — and if you've ever been near a cod when it has got a bit high you'll have some sympathy with the Taters' point of view. They started attacking the Cod People, who responded by building a huge wire mesh fence running north-to-south along the western edge of their domain to shut out the Taters. This restored the status quo, and the two races might have eventually learned to co-exist in peace — but at this point Nature played a grim jest. (I don't know if it was as grim as some of my jests, but it was pretty nasty.)

At this crucial point in time — the Earth tilted on its axis! It flopped over by 23½ degrees.

Those of you who have logical, trained, scientific minds will — as well as quietly vomiting into your convention booklet envelopes — have leaped ahead of me at this point, and realised the significance of the 23½ degree angle I marked on Diagram A.

The effect was cataclysmic! Even bigger, would you believe, than the upheaval caused by the recent reorganisation of the BSFA!

All the water that had been covering Eastern England swilled away into the North Sea, leaving the poor Cod People flopping about in puddles dying horrible and protracted deaths. And, to add insult to injury, all the Taters were thrown with great force against the wire mesh fence ... were sliced up by it ... and showered down on top of the dying Cod People in the form of long rectangular prisms.

The vision is almost too horrible to contemplate — two noble and once-proud races wiped out in the twinkling of an eye, their pitiful remains inextricably mixed up together.

At that stage, Nature — as though shamed by the mute reproaches of her own gory handiwork — drew a shroud of ice and snow over the scene of carnage. (What a pity that *Stirring Science Stories* had to cease publication — I could have sold this stuff to them for a *fortune!*) The workings of Nature's cover-up job are explained in Diagram C. The Earth had tilted by 23½ degrees, but it was done with such a jolt that the polar ice cap skidded on a bit further — rather like a fried egg in a new non-stick frying pan — and ended up with its bottom edge across the southern part of England. The line marking the lower limit of the ice cap — as can best be shown on Diagram B — passes, *not without significance,* exactly through Bermondsey. (Actually, it passes through the backroom of a Chinese take-away in Peckham, but we've already decided not to go into that. I got into enough trouble through going into the backroom of the Bangla-Desh in Newcastle.)

What, you must be asking, is the next startling revelation in this tale of Earth in the throes of cosmic upheaval?

Well, I'll tell you — otherwise there wouldn't be much point in me sitting up here like a berk when I could be in the bar enjoying myself. The next thing that happened was that a race of alien beings descended from the stars and, because they came from a very chilly planet, settled around the North Pole. Von Donegan has already dealt extensively with these invaders, whom he dubbed Icekimoes, in his book *The Skateboards of the Gods* — but that is a slightly misleading title, because the Icekimoes actually went around in huge salt-powered sleds.

These bizarre vehicles, which could only have been

the product of an alien mind, operated on an ingenious principle. Each one had a large salt shaker mounted in front of it. The salt was shaken down onto the ice, which promptly melted, creating a small hill which the sled slid down — and the process was continuously repeated. Ah, I can see that the technically-minded people in the audience are objecting to this notion on sound engineering principles — and I know what your objection is. You're saying the sleds would never be able to carry enough salt to go any distance. Well, the Icekimoes thought of that, naturally, and they positioned salt dumps, for refueling, all over their territories, which extended to the southern extremities of the ice cap.

However, the millennia rolled onwards inexorably, the ice cap retreated from England and reformed in its proper place, and the enigmatic Icekimoes withdrew from the stage of world history to be lost forever in the swirling Arctic snows. (You know, this stuff is too good for *Stirring Science Stories* — if I polished it up a bit I bet I could flog it to *Reader's Digest*. It would look well in there along with all those articles about how getting cancer is actually quite enjoyable. My favorite article from *Reader's Digest* was the one entitled "New Hope for the Dead.")

As I was saying, the Icekimoes gradually disappeared, leaving no traces of their existence except for numerous mounds of salt all over the place — but then a new lot of alien invaders came up from the south. Little is known about this second wave of invaders, partly because Von Donegan hasn't had time to cook up much archaeological evidence about them, partly because their empire was confined to areas of the world where the top layer was composed of limestone or chalk. The reason for this seemingly arbitrary limit to their movements is that they used vehicles which were even more ingenious than salt-powered sleds — they used vinegar-powered hovercraft!

Ancient hieroglyphs on the walls of caves near Dover — which Von Donegan is hoping to finish carving before he goes on his holidays next month — clearly show these beings sitting on their little hovercraft, which worked by spraying acetic acid on the chalky ground and floating on the clouds of carbon dioxide which were given off as a result. He gave them the name of Sarsons — not to be confused with Saracens — because their fuel was remarkably similar to a well-known brand of vinegar.

For a brief period the Sarsons ranged over that part of Britain which has a top stratum of chalk or limestone, an area whose eastern edge is a fairly straight line running downwards from Newcastle through . . . you've guessed it! . . . the back room of the Chinese take-away in Peckham High Street.

And there you have it! The Bermondsey Triangle clearly defined, for all to see!

In case you haven't already worked it out, I should explain that the Sarsons stayed in Britain for only a short time, because a general Ice Age was coming and their technology wasn't sufficiently advanced to enable them to invent a satisfactory anti-freeze for their vinegar. They retreated to the south, the Ice Age held sway for thousands of years, and when the glaciers finally retreated Homo Sapiens had at last appeared on the scene. Who said "Bloody near time!" down at the back there?

Anyway, life was very difficult at first for this puny hairless creature with his ineffectual teeth — this was long before the National Health Service provided him with wigs and stainless steel dentures for next to nothing. It was even before the Biblical scribes had started to write screenplays for Charlton Heston, and early man would have died away in short order had he not found the one place on Earth where survival was easy. Preserved in the permafrost of the Bermondsey Triangle was a tectonic plate of fish and chips, ready-sprinkled with salt and vinegar.

When conditions were too harsh for intelligent life throughout the rest of the world, the fish-and-chip mines of the Bermondsey Triangle were supporting thriving communities of well-nourished human beings, who — once or twice a year — gathered at the largest diggings to replenish their supplies and to give thanks to their deities.

Small wonder, then, that deep-rooted racial memories cause some of their descendants to flock to the same places and go through half-understood rituals. Large numbers of them cram themselves into small rooms at night and drink vast amounts of alcoholic liquor, much to the annoyance of those in neighbouring rooms — thus acting out the role of the Cod People getting tanked up on codswallop and enraging the Taters.

Many small blocks of duplicated paper are thrown around, an obvious re-enactment of the original showering of the area with sliced-up Taters. And a tall, priestly, imposing figure, ceremonially robed, or sometimes ceremonially disrobed, passes among the pilgrims, distributing pork pies which are symbolic of — and nearly as old as — the primaeval fish and chips.

Von Donegan believes that the large amounts of alcohol drunk during the day at these strange congresses represent the acetic acid which the Sarsons sprinkled over everything from their hovercraft — which reminds me that I have left a large vinegar-and-tonic out in the bar...

PYROTECHNICS

This column, written more than 30 years ago, remains the one which gives me the most pleasure to re-read. It is the most evocative and nostalgic, perhaps because of the ambiance of Fireworks Night. Certainly, the occasion provided a perfect opportunity to bring all of the characters of Irish Fandom together on the stage and show them in action. It is sad to reflect that, because of the Northern Ireland situation, the authorities had to ban fireworks and therefore Halloween can no longer be celebrated in the way I described here, in the winter of 1954...

* * *

On Saturday, October 30, the city of Belfast held its Halloween celebrations. [Note: this is the Irish equivalent of Guy Fawkes day.] There was the usual number of explosive sounds and bright flashes of light extending into the small hours of Sunday morning. By Sunday night the last newly neurotic cat had descended from the trees and all but the most cautious of old ladies had removed the plugs from the ears of their pet canaries. By Monday the city had relapsed into its normal, quietly humdrum existence...

Heh! Heh! Heh!

We held our display on Tuesday night.

At a quarter to eight George Charters arrived and I let him in. He was wearing a bulky tweed coat and a bulky tweed cap, an outfit which makes him look rather like a hairy mammoth with herring-bone skin. "Ah, there you are," he shouted. "I'm going to let you and the rest have it. I'm in form for bloodshed. Just let me get at yiz — I'm dangerous tonight."

"Wait a minute, George," I said, "we won't be playing Ghoodminton for a while yet — we're having a fireworks display first."

"That's a pity," he replied, "I was looking forward to a friendly game." We went out to the back where the others were gathered watching Walter let off a few Fairy Sparklers for the benefit of his small daughter and two of her playmates. We arrived just in time to hear the last of an argument betwen him and James. James had tied two threepenny rockets together and fixed a sparkler onto the bottom of the sticks. Walt had said that this contraption would rise no higher than a single rocket, which remark had caused James to fall back on his BIS jargon in indignant denial. He spouted a lot of highly technical data and knelt to ignite his masterpiece. He lit the sparkler and the two fuses and leapt back, glancing resentfully at the layer of slightly leaky cloud a mere two thousand feet up. He resigned himself to losing sight of the rocket before it really got going.

We all stood there in the damp darkness — waiting. The sparkler burned merrily inside the milk bottle for about three minutes and then went out. "Stand back," warned James as we closed in a bit. "It will go thundering skywards any second now." About a minute later the slightly touched paper was all consumed and the rockets began to blast. They thundered skywards for about ten feet, faltered, keeled over and wobbled drunkenly along the ground for a short distance. They barely cleared a fence and expired fitfully in somebody's back garden.

We could see that James was shaken, that his faith in rocketry was shattered, so nobody spoke. We just laughed.

"Let's get on with the other stuff," said Walter. "What else have we?"

As I told him about my deadly arsenal of Atomic Crashers and Little Demons, and John Berry babbled enthusiastically about the blast areas and flame-throwing abilities of his stuff, it seemed to me that Walter's face paled slightly. "I've been thinking," he announced after a few moments. "There isn't much space here—let's all go round to my father's house." This seemed a good idea so we set off. As I passed James he was staring at the point where his rocket had disappeared and muttering, "The fools! The poor fools! They'll never reach the Moon."

With rustling raincoats and squelching shoes we trooped along through the fine drizzle to a house several quiet streets away. Walter opened the front gate and ushered us all in; for some reason he seemed happier now, and placed us at the side of the house with a severe injunction to keep quiet. We huddled against the gable while Walter brought Carol and the other two little girls to the front door and rang the bell. We listened with bated breath as he explained how, out of the goodness of his kindly heart, he wanted to treat the children to a few fireworks. He reappeared and we trudged round to the back.

I saw the rain-blurred faces of Walter's father and mother peering out of a side window as Walter went by with his silent retinue of small children. The faces began to withdraw, then reappeared hurriedly as Madeleine Willis and my wife

Sadie passed into their ken. They remained there in silent
bewilderment as James and his fiancee Peggy went by,
closely followed by John, then me. They drew back
instinctively as George lumbered past in the rear in his bulky
tweed overcoat and bulky tweed cap. I felt sorry for those
faces.

To begin the display we shot off a few rockets in their
natural state. These flew quite well but they all seemed to fly
in the one direction — towards a dimly seen house in the row
whose back gardens abutted on the one we were in, separated
from us by a tennis court. After we had tired of this we began
the second part of the show — the aerodynamic section. I had
brought some of the flying squibs known as "Flying Imps"
and glued wings onto them, making them look like tiny V2s.
I felt proud of these little spaceships for they flew perfectly
although the weight of the wings always brought them down
again. Funnily enough, these too all landed on or around the
same house. I became distincly aware of slight stirrings of life
from the direction of this ill-fated building, but it didn't seem
worth mentioning.

The next item was the ascent of John's Viking. He had
sawn the stick off a shilling rocket and glued on balsa wood
wings and painted it in big black and white checks. It was
lovely looking. We lit it and stood back. At that moment we
heard an aeroplane passing over very high and somebody
suggested trying to bring it down, somebody else began to
hum "Dragnet" and I heard Walter muttering something
about lighting the blue paper and retiring from fandom. At
that moment the Viking took off. It was magnificent the way
it climbed on a pillar of blinding incandescence just the way
they do in the books. Everybody agreed afterwards that it
was the best thing in the show. There was only one thing
wrong. John must have made one of the wings heavier than

the others because pretty high up the rocket leaned to one side and turned over, still blasting away. I looked round for a shovel with the vague idea of digging a slit trench, but I need not have worried — it nosedived the same house as before.

Next I let off some of my high explosive ones but only a couple of them banged and Walter's father came out to see what was happening. He looked at his garden, which we had reduced to a pretty fair imitation of Flanders. I heard him say, "This is a good place to let them off," and he wasn't even *slightly* sarcastic. Honest.

Sadie and Madeleine were beginning to get bored with the poor performance of the bangers so they called for something new. James must have been still carrying the mental scars of his earlier brush with the force of gravity, for he suggested tying two rockets together so that they faced in opposite directions... "Let them lie there and *strain.*" This sadistic idea was quashed by John, who suggested tying four rockets together and holding them with pliers until they were all firing. James countered this by pointing out that we had no parachute to wear "just in case."

We finally decided to tie an Atomic Crasher onto a rocket. Now, I have a theory about these particular squibs. I bought them in one bundle and I think that, by some mistake in the factory, the first six I lit had had no explosive in them. Also I think that all the powder that should have gone into them went into number seven. As luck would have it that was the one we put on the rocket. While we were sellotaping it on, James, who was beginning to recover his faith, worked out the chances of a good flight. "A 3d rocket and a 1d banger... hmmm! That's a pretty good lift — a three to one ratio." Getting even more hopeful, he said we might even break the sound barrier. I never heard of anything sillier — for supersonic flight you need a sixpenny rocket at least.

Anyway I lit the Atomic Crasher, waited a few seconds, and then lit the rocket. It went up at a terrific velocity. It had achieved quite a fair height when the weight of the banger pulled it over to one side. It turned and zoomed downwards, its trail of sparks now reinforced by those from the squib. It disappeared from view behind a hedge, but we could see that it had landed...yes, that's right...fair and square in the backyard of the same house. Exactly at the moment of impact the Atomic Crasher exploded. I saw the intervening hedge limned with crimson flame and the ground shook below our feet. Everybody burst out laughing except me — I had belatedly remembered that there had been somebody moving out there. Somebody in our group said in a stricken voice, "My Ghod! The Russkis have got in first." James said, "The lights are going out all over town." When our ears stopped ringing we realised that every dog for miles around was appealing in a loud voice to its canine Ghu to come and save it. Suddenly through the sounds in my head and the, I suspect, slightly hysterical laughter and the yammering of the dogs I heard what I had been dreading to hear...

From the direction of that last appalling detonation, borne on the rain-laden night air, there came faint piteous cries.

I don't know what the poor devil was trying to say but he certainly sounded as if he was in a bad way. My sleep is still haunted by his faint bleats of bewilderment mingled with pure fear and helpless, impotent anger. James, who was by this time once more his old devil-may-care self, gleefully whispered, "That gap in that row of houses wasn't there before."

The more prudent of us decided that we had better move on before the police cars arrived, so we gathered our gear and set off back to Walter's. As we were walking back I found a Flying Imp in my pocket so I let it off in the street.

I can't remember much about the ensuing few seconds but John has covered it for me...

* * *

[John Berry writing: I noticed that Bob was absent. I looked round, and saw him bending down by a front gate. I hurried on, presuming he was trying to complete the night's destruction by blowing up the gate with his last Atomic Crasher. Seconds later I heard a hissing noise, followed by a cry of frustration. I looked round, startled. There was Bob, eyes protruding, cheeks puffed out, his feet a sheer blur of slashing movement. He flashed past, coat tails akimbo, hotly pursued by a Flying Imp with a long comet-like tail. The nose of the Imp was about 2½" from Bob's nether regions. I yelled to the crowd, and they parted respectfully to make way for the strange procession. There was a final devastating explosion, then silence and utter darkness. We pulled Bob from the hedge, carefully removing the Imp. Sadie retrieved his collar and tie from a nearby lamp-post. We eventually managed to calm him down, none the worse for his impulsive flight.]

* * *

[Bob Shaw Ctd.] Thank you, John. Personally I refuse to believe that I could ever behave in such an undignified manner, but let the readers judge for themselves. See the way when anybody makes a crack at me I just laugh?

Back at Walter's I planted my remaining banger in the damp earth and lit it. To tell the truth I was still thinking about that unknown soul whose evening reverie had been so rudely shattered ... that's how I failed to notice that the blue paper had broken off this one. I absent-mindedly touched the match to it and found to my horror that I was squatting (off balance too) in a shower of sparks from a prematurely exploding Atomic Crasher. Gibbering horribly with un-diluted fear I took off down the path, travelling about six inches above the ground. I crashed through the world record for the twenty yards, the sound barrier and several ranks of grinning fans and femmes. I was proud of that dash — it made me feel like one of the Unkillables in *Final Blackout*. Gritting my teeth to keep my heart from bouncing out onto the ground, I turned to witness the explosion of the Hell-Bomb.

It went... "phhht."

A dimly seen object that I had taken to be a huge pile of dustbins painted in zig-zag camouflage turned out to be George Charters in his bulky tweed coat and cap. It said, in a patient voice, "Now will you go up and play Ghoodminton?"

So we all went in for friendly, safe, *predictable* Ghoodminton.

AD ASTRA?

At the age of 14 I decided to become an astronomer.

As a first step in achieving this ambition, I read every book on the subject in the public library at the rate of one or two a week. This second-hand stargazing was satisfying enough for some months, but, as time wore on, it became apparent that a telescope of one's own was *de rigueur* for up-and-coming astronomers.

The concentrated reading course had taught me quite a bit about astronomical instruments and I was able to decide at once that the best one for my purpose would be a five-inch telescope, which, in non-technical language, is a telescope which measures five inches across the fat end. Unfortunately, although the library books had dealt very thoroughly with matters like focal lengths, chromatic aberration and altazimuth mountings, they had been completely mute on the subject of prices. There was, as I was later to learn, a very good reason for this omission. A first-class five-inch telescope with accessories can easily cost several hundred pounds, and as the theme of most authors was, "How foolish it is to waste money on going to the cinema when you can

survey the limitless splendours of the Universe for nothing!"
they were understandably reluctant to descend to the vulgar
financial details. However, I was unaware of all this at the
time, and in the absence of guidance estimated a price by
myself. The calculation was quite simple — I had once owned
a telescope measuring about one inch across which had cost
me three shillings: the one I wanted to buy was five times
thicker and therefore should cost three shillings multiplied
by five, equals fifteen shillings. Allowing a bit extra for
inflation I reckoned that if I raised eighteen shillings I would
be in a position to put up a serious challenge to Armagh
Observatory.

Some weeks later — slightly weakened by total abstinence
from regular items of diet such as Nutty Nibs and Jap
Dessert, but filled with an unbearably delicious sense of
anticipation — I cycled downtown on a brisk Saturday
morning to purchase a telescope, with almost a pound safely
buttoned in my hip pocket. Saving the money had been hard
work so I decided not actually to go into the first instrument
maker's shop I came to in case he hadn't got a five-inch
telescope in stock and talked me into buying a less powerful
four-inch, or even a miserable little three-inch. Accordingly,
I went round all the instrument makers and after hours of
studying their window displays and peering in through their
doors began to feel slightly disappointed. None of them
seemed to *have* any decent-sized telescopes, and I could hear
in my imagination the familiar phrase, "Oh, we'd have to
send away to England for that."

Finally dusk began to fall and, as it was bitterly cold and
lunchtime was several hours past, I decided to compromise.
One of the shops had a skimpy little thing of not more than
two inches diameter in the window and although it was a
pale imitation of what I wanted it would at least get me

cracking on the limitless splendours of the universe that very evening. The money left over after buying it, I consoled myself, would be a good start towards the price of a proper telescope.

The thin, meticulously neat, severe-looking man behind the counter did not look particularly pleased to see me. He jerked his head enquiringly and went on polishing a row of expensive cameras.

"I'm interested in the telescope you have in the window."

He stopped polishing and fixed a cold gaze on my cycle clips. I withstood the scrutiny confidently, knowing the cycle clips were as good as money could buy. I decided to let him know that here was a fellow expert on precision instruments.

"It's got an object glass of about two inches," I said, realising it might be a good idea to chat about technical details for a while, and only after he had seen that I knew something about telescopes bring up the subject of price.

"It's thirty-two pounds ten," he said with a complete lack of finesse or preamble, and went right back to polishing the cameras.

The blow did not hit me right away. I sneered at the back of his head a couple of times, then dashed out of the shop with two objectives in mind — to buy a telescope before closing time and to spread the word around the trade that one of its members was trying to sell six-shilling telescopes for thirty-two pounds ten. Half an hour later I was slowly cycling homewards, sickened by the discovery that they were all in it together. It seemed as if I was shut off from the stars as effectively as if huge steel shutters had sprung up from behind the Castlereagh Hills on one side and the Black Mountain on the other and had clanged together overhead.

The despair lasted several days, then, with a resurgence of hope, I realised what had to be done. It was all so simple. If the people who sold brand new telescopes had formed a price ring the thing was to pick up a second-hand instrument from some friendly old junk dealer who had no idea of its current market value. Within a week I had developed a deep and implacable hatred for friendly old junk dealers — obviously somebody had told them what the telescope makers were up to and the unscrupulous rogues had pushed their own prices up to within shillings of the brand-new prices. The stars would have to wait, but this time the situation didn't seem quite so hopeless. I couldn't believe that junk dealers would be as well organised as instrument makers and there was always the chance that one day one of them would make a mistake.

Then began a phase of my life which lasted several years and gave me an unrivalled knowledge of Belfast's second-hand shops, even those in distant quarters of the city. On Saturdays and lunch times and holidays I spent my time checking the dingy little shops, going in hopefully each time a new telescope appeared, coming out in renewed despair on hearing the price. Not once during those years did a friendly old junk dealer make a mistake. They maintained the price barrier which separated me from the distant untrodden reaches of the universe as though it was all part of a gigantic plot.

Fruitless though the search was, it produced an occasional memorable experience. One Saturday afternoon I was prowling through the darker corners of Smithfield Market when I discerned a tiny brass object which I immediately recognised as being the eye-piece of a fairly large telescope. It was completely useless to me, but out of sheer force of habit, I asked the price from the old woman in charge. After sizing me up cheerfully she announced that it was seven and sixpence. Her business sense must have been remarkably good for I had about eight shillings in my pocket at that moment, and immediately said I would buy. There was absolutely nothing I could do with the eye-piece of course, but it was the first thing in the telescope line that had come into my price range, and I had to have it. I had come a long way from that first morning when I set out to buy a five-inch telescope.

The old lady knew the object was only an eye-piece from an instrument perhaps six-foot long but she had no way of knowing that I too fully understood this, and, when she saw my obvious delight at the price, seemed to feel an unprofessional pang of remorse. She stood for a while as greed battled with guilt, then slowly handed the tube over and took my money. As I was going out through the door she emitted a faint strangling sound which made me look back, and I realised she was going to speak.

"You know," she finally ground out, "there's a piece missing."

I nodded. Having gone that far she had made peace with her conscience and we parted in a glow of mutual satisfaction. Surprisingly enough, my money was not altogether wasted because I began to pick up other vaguely telescopic items in the form of magnifying glasses and spectacle lenses, and discovered that it was possible to *make* telescopes — after a fashion, that is. My first one was constructed from a piece of lead piping, made stars look like little balls of illuminated candy floss, and was so heavy that when I let it fall from the bedroom window one night it woke half the street and threw one of my father's dogs into some kind of fit.

That was the first occasion on which I became aware of a rather strange fact. Astronomy was presumably the quietest and most respectable pursuit any teenager could be expected to take up, but every time I got into my stride people and small animals kicked up hell. There was the time I built a telescope with a wooden tube and made the marvellous discovery that some of the tiles on our roof could be slid out of the way, leaving a hole big enough to poke the telescope through from the attic. I began work on a suitable telescope mounting right away but during the first half hour our front door was almost pounded down by panic-stricken passers-by coming to warn us that our roof was collapsing. So great was the consternation caused by my private observatory that one of the first people to call was an old lady who hadn't spoken to any of us for years, not since the day my younger brother, with the ruthless ease of a Japanese sniper, had annihilated her row of prize tulips with his air rifle. (From her back garden she had seen the flowers fold over, one by one, apparently without reason, and had given such a heart-rending scream that my brother vowed never again to shoot anything but birds and cats.) Anyway, I was forced to abandon the eyrie.

In between tours of junk shops I persevered with telescope-building and in the process learned a lot about the science of optics. I learned to calculate the magnification obtained by even the most complicated lens system, but preferred the simpler method of direct measurement. To find out how strong a telescope is, one looks through it at a brick wall and keeps the other eye open, with the result that large bricks and small bricks are seen superimposed on each other. A count of the number of small bricks that fit into a big brick gives the instrument's magnification.

The snag with this method was that every now and again the brick would be blotted out by a sudden flurry of movement and I would find myself staring at the vastly magnified and outraged face of a fat middle-aged woman.

Sometimes the fat middle-aged woman gathered an excited knot of other fat middle-aged women who stood around, arms crossed protectively over their bosoms, muttering among themselves and staring in disquiet at my bedroom window. I always cringed back, appalled, wondering what I could say to my parents if the police or a deputation from the Church arrived at the door.

Finally, after about five years, I acquired a reasonable telescope. Not the five-inch job I had set out to buy on that fateful Saturday morning — that was still beyond my pocket — but a reasonable telescope, nevertheless.

Anybody who has even a superficial understanding of the workings of the human brain inside the human bonce will guess what happened next. I was disappointed. During those five years the anticipated pleasures of owning an astronomical telescope had multiplied themselves in my mind to a point which could not have been satisfied by all the resources of a modern observatory. Prolonged re-reading of the poetic astronomy books of people like Garrett P. Serviss (remember his early science fiction?) had convinced me that putting my eye to a telescope would transport me to another plane of existence in which the grey realities of mundane life would be replaced by a wonderland of celestial jewels, vari-coloured and mind-drinking; clusters like fireflies tangled in silver braid; glowing nebulae among whose filaments the imagination could wander for ever and ever.

Of course, all I saw were quivering and meaningless specks of light, and I got rid of the telescope within a few weeks.

And yet, the years-long search was not wasted. Now, twenty years further on, I still occasionally dream that I have found a friendly old junk dealer who doesn't know the price of telescopes. I smell the dust in his shop, I see the uncomprehending china dogs, I experience the limits of intellectual delight as I carry the solid, heavy instrument out into the street — moving towards a beautiful future which can never exist.

You couldn't buy dreams like that.

THE MAN IN THE GREY
FLANNEL TOGA

One evening last winter while glancing through the *Radio Times* I discovered that the BBC was going to give *Julius Caesar* the full treatment in about half an hour's time. The discovery of and the imminence of this veritable pearl sent me into a state of near oysteria. I dashed out and purchased two pint bottles of Amber Ale, got the fire well stoked up, equipped myself with glass, bottle opener, pipe, tobacco, and slippers, and settled down in an armchair before the TV set. Once that TV of ours gets into your chair nothing will shift it.

The play opened in a rather unfamiliar manner — nothing but grey mist and a strange, eerie silence. I was explaining to Sadie that I didn't care much for the liberties the BBC had taken with the original settings when she noticed that the set wasn't switched on. Once that was done I began to enjoy the show. Everything went well until the third act, then my memory began to stir uneasily, dredging up fragmentary glimpses of the past...

Suddenly it was all there. Of *course*. How could I have forgotten the sheer misery of my first and last taste of the footlights' glare? This was the play I had been forced to take part in during my first year at the Technical High School. Gradually the sound and fury of the BBC version began to recede as the events of that ghastly evening came crowding back . . .

The English teacher in charge of the production was an athletic tweedy man with a square, angry face. His name was Carson and he was feared throughout the first year sections because, according to rumour, he had been known, when enraged, to demolish even the largest boys by applying a sort of wrestling submission hold known as the Corkscrew. This involved putting his left arm round your neck, catching the short hairs of your temple in his right hand, and winding them like an old gramophone. Nobody had ever actually *seen* Carson do this but we all went in dread of suddenly being given the Corkscrew.

Actually I shouldn't have been in the play at all. In fact, the only reason for the whole business was that Carson, like so many short-tempered people, believed himself to be something of a humourist. He had written a take-off of *Julius Caesar* for the end-of-term social and had realised at the last moment that all the clever bits, such as the assassination scene in which the conspirators used tommy guns, would not be appreciated by the rabble. Accordingly he had decided to do the play seriously to show us what the real thing was like, and had cast third- and fourth-year students in the major parts.

In English class one day I was laboriously making carbon copies of my class magazine, known for some forgotten and unguessable reason as "Le Hibou and Ku Klux Klan Journal," when Carson appeared beside me and saw what I was doing. I cowered back, covering my temples, but to my surprise he took the matter quite well. After a public enquiry into the policies and circulation figures of my magazine, which left the rest of the class in stitches, he asked whether my evident interest in the Arts included any desire to be a Thespian.

I had a vague idea that the word meant something peculiar and mumbled incoherently about being too young.

Carson didn't seem to notice. He handed me a copy of *Julius Caesar,* showed me my part, which consisted of two lines in Act 3, and told me to show up at rehearsals that evening. Some of the boys who sat nearby almost became ill with senseless laughter — this was going to be something to talk about for years.

As it turned out I only had to attend one rehearsal, due to being conscripted so late, and things went so well at it that I became reconciled with the idea of being an actor. One serious snag was the obvious impossibility of producing reasonable facsimiles of Roman army uniforms, but Carson had got round this by dressing everybody, even Mark Antony and Pompey, in togas. These consisted of lengthy pieces of curtain material borrowed from the Art classrooms. An elderly teacher by the name of Miss Anderson fitted them on the boys with safety pins.

There was not enough material on hand to provide me with a toga so I did my bit in my ordinary clothes, which at that particular time consisted of shapeless grey flannels and an ex-ARP jacket. Before I went on Miss Anderson provided me with a spear and a circular cardboard shield.

Just as I was ready to make my entrance Carson buttonholed me. "Listen, Shaw," he said, "I want you to speak up. Don't mumble. Your part is small but it is important that the audience hear what you say, so speak up. And keep your shield on your upstage arm to give them the full benefit of your gallant warrior's physique."

I ignored the sarcasm and did all I was told and it felt pretty good. I came off fired with enthusiasm — perhaps this was the start of a new career. Still in this mood I told Miss Anderson that I was going to do away with the circular target, which was most un-Roman, and was going to make a proper semi-cylindrical shield. She thought that would be very nice and agreed rather lugubriously to make me a sort of tunic and skirt to wear. I could see my performance being described as "a little gem" in the school magazine.

On the big night I got down to the school early and smuggled my shield into the dressing rooms. Most of the other boys were there already wearing their togas and stamping their feet with the cold. It was November and the dressing rooms were like gloomy iceboxes. Our breaths filled the place with a faint fog.

After some enquiries I found out that Miss Anderson had left my outfit in a paper bag in the cupboard. I brought it out, took off my clothes, and then discovered to my horror that Miss Anderson's idea of a Roman soldier's uniform was a grey silk thing with thin shoulder straps and a plunging neckline. I put it on and found that it came down just far enough to cover my trunks and no more. When the shout of laughter went up from the others I developed a sneaking suspicion that Miss Anderson had given up trying to make anything and had given me an old petticoat. Mark Antony began talking in a high-pitched voice, prodding me with his rubber dagger, and finally tried to make me waltz with him. I was saved by the arrival of Carson.

"Unhand that maiden, Marcus Antonius," he said. Carson loved to use the old form of words and names — he was a sort of ycleptomaniac. Luckily, as the play was about to commence, he had no time for further comment on my costume and I suddenly found myself alone in the dressing room. I decided not to wait in the wings with the others and slumped down in a corner to wait my turn.

An hour later, when it came, I had turned a mottled blue with touches of burgundy here and there. I was practically unable to speak. Getting through the crush in the wings was easy; I just kept putting my hand on bare arms and the crowd melted before me. It was a bit like the scene where Quasimodo frightens the people going up the cathedral steps.

Somehow I got onto the stage, husked my two lines about the approach of some army, and ran off. I found out afterwards from boys who had been there with their parents that I had carried my huge semi-cylindrical shield on my downstage arm and, as well as not hearing me, the audience hadn't even *seen* me. Into the bargain I was shivering so much that the flabby point of my spear had almost leapt off the stick.

Back in the throng I saw Carson bearing down on me with a look of unbridled hatred on his face. I clapped my hands over my temples, gave a despairing whimper, and clawed my way into the dressing room. I threw on my trousers and ARP jacket over my costume and fled through another door.

The next day in class Carson didn't speak to me. Now that I think of it, I don't believe he ever spoke to me again.

TEN YEARS, BUT
NOT DECAYED

 W ell, here we are — back in the good old Metropole — the only hotel in England that's big enough to house a modern-day SF convention. And it is *big*, isn't it? I was watching an SF movie last night and I was almost going to complain about the quality of the colour. All the actors' faces were very pink — and it wasn't only because the script was by George Lucas. Then it dawned on me it was due to the size of the auditorium. I was so far from the screen that the light from it was red-shifted!

And then there are all the corridors. You have to go through corridors to get to the corridors. I don't know why it is but all convention hotels are exceptionally well endowed with corridors. Even the ones that look quite small on the outside have these miles and miles of featureless corridors and passages which take you round and round the building, and sometimes deposit you in the car park. The Station Hotel in Glasgow is a particularly bad case. Fans have checked in at conventions there and have never been heard of again. I would have got lost many times in the last few years if it wasn't for the fact that I have discovered a good landmark in the Station Hotel. It's that half-eaten pork pie which sits on the window sill on the south side of the fourth floor. When I'm filling in my hotel booking form I always put in a special request for a room near the pork pie.

And did you ever notice that your room in these big sprawling hotels is always as far away from the lift as it can get? I have worked out a mathematical expression for this (Terry Hill published it recently in *Microwave*). If the sign opposite the lift says "Room X to Room Y," then your room number wil be $(X + Y)/2$.

I'm rambling on a bit about corridors, but I feel it's an important subject for convention-goers, because all this space devoted to corridors has an unfortunate side-effect. There's hardly any room left for rooms! The Metropole is okay, but I've been in convention hotels which were designed by the same chap who did the Black Hole of Calcutta. At my last con the toilet in the room was so small that you had to make up your mind what you were going to do before you went in. The fridge in the room was so small that when you made ice cubes the expansion of the water pushed the door open.

And what makes the room problem even worse is that every hotel has *two* sets of corridors. There are the ordinary corridors that we use — and then there are the special secret corridors that the staff use. Did you ever open one of those doors marked "STAFF ONLY"? Everything is made of concrete in there. It's a sort of alternate universe. The entire hotel is duplicated in concrete behind those doors for the benefit of the staff only. I find it all a bit alarming. Why do they need it? There's never anybody in there. The cleaners are always to be found in the ordinary corridors, transferring each room's set of damp towels to the next room. Perhaps one of these years I'll do a proper scientific investigation of this thing and let you know the results.

I should repeat that I'm not criticising the Metropole. They treat SF fans with respect here. I think it's humiliating in the Royal Angus in Birmingham the way the fans can hardly get saying goodbye to each other at the end of a convention because of the staff carrying the furniture back in. When you check in at the Metropole there's none of this business of, "Good morning, sir, are you with the SF convention — or are you having a room with carpets?"

Anyway — on to the talk! I gave my first Serious Scientific Talk at the Newcastle Eastercon in 1974, which means that this is my tenth anniversary. Ten years on the frontiers of knowledge, going far beyond the boundaries of science and good taste alike, inspiring scientists and laymen and fans of *Space: 1999* with respect and laughter and hatred — though not necessarily in that order.

This year, instead of taking one topic and subjecting it to my usual rigorous scientific analysis, I have decided to review the advances that have been made in the last decade in the fields of science and science fiction. And what a decade of progress and achievement it has been! Isaac Asimov came out with *Foundation's Edge,* which proved that he has lost none of the literary attributes which made him famous back in the Forties. Scientists have launched into space an infra-red telescope which is so sensitive, they claim, that it can detect the heat from a cricket ball at a range of 200,000 miles.

I have to admit, though, that I'm a bit worried about that one. I mean, who the hell *put* that warm cricket ball up there? Scientists have a thing about cricket, you know. It all dates back to the time when Einstein made that ridiculous statement, which I have mentioned before, that $E = MCC$.

The Marylebone Cricket Club issued an immediate denial, of course, but the rumour still persists. And when I was a reporter with the *Belfast Telegraph* many years ago I had to write a piece about a local research institute having put in a new electron microscope. The scientists in charge issued a press release which boasted how powerful the instrument was — and guess what they gave for an example! Did they tell us how large it would make a human hair look? Did they say how large it would make a blood cell look? Nope! They told what the effect would be if you looked through it at a *cricket pitch!* At the time I dismissed it as inept popular science writing on their part, but now this mysterious warm cricket ball has shown up 200,000 miles out in space. Something else I'll have to look into...

Another big technological advance of the last decade has been the advent of the quartz-powered watch. Practically all the watches and clocks in the shops these days are powered by quartz, but I'm happy to report that my German-Irish colleague, Von Donegan, has gone one step further. He has invented a watch which is powered by pints! It is, of course, only half the size of a quartz watch, and runs off a little Guinness reservoir which the wearer straps to his back. It gives you all kinds of useful data — British double summer time, Irish double whiskey time, etc. — but, not content with that, Von Donegan is working on an advanced model. In the MkII watch the Guinness flows into *him* and the watch operates off his breath. The main difficulty is in maintaining a steady flow of gaseous alcohol into the watch, but Von Donegan tells me he has it almost licked. Just a few hiccups to eliminate...

Von Donegan is also reported to be working on a supermarket trolley which will travel in a straight line, and I wish him every success with it. When I go into a supermarket to buy just one or two small items I refuse to struggle with one of those lumbering great trolleys. I would feel stupid wheeling a huge trolley around with only a toothbrush in it, fighting to keep it going straight, but on the other hand I feel equally stupid doing the funny walk. You know the one you have to do when you've picked up a small item ... you can feel the security cameras on you ... and the eyes of the store detectives ... and you have to carry it around in a way which proclaims to all and sundry that you're not going to steal it. The Honest Man's Mince, I call it. You're trying to broadcast a signal which says, "Look! It's obvious I'm going to pay for this at the check-out." But the trouble is you tend to look more like John Inman, broadcasting a different kind of a signal, and you risk getting touched up between the gondolas.

I have nothing against homosexuality, I hasten to add. In fact I think it's a very good idea — for women. Suppose some kind of a miracle took place and I got transformed into a woman ... If I were dozing in an armchair at home and a fairy appeared and turned me into a woman ... I can see myself wakening up with a start and saying, "My goodness — I must have dropped off!" If that happened I would immediately become a homosexual, because homosexual women get to go to bed with other women, and it's all very nice. But you just try being a homosexual when you're a *man*. You've to go to bed with other men and have awful things done to you.

Where was I? I seem to have deviated. I had just dealt with all the scientific advances of the last ten years and was about to turn my attention to science fiction and fantasy. I'm not going to make the mistake of trying to predict what science will do in the next ten years. The only safe prediction one can make is that all predictions will be proved wrong. That's why

I get a bit annoyed every time a popular journal decides to start plugging old Nostradamus.

A Nostradamus freak was trying to convert me recently, and he showed me some of the quatrains and said, "Look at the incredible way he predicted Hitler." Reluctantly impressed, I read the relevant page, then said, "Wait a minute! This is about somebody called *Hister*. There's no mention of Hitler in here." The freak looked impatient and said, "It obviously *means* Hitler. He just got one letter wrong — an S instead of an L." I said, "But that would make it Hilter. Who the hell was Hilter? I never heard of anybody called Hilter." The Nostradamus fan snatched the book away and muttered something about sour grapes and me having the nerve to call myself a science fiction writer when I wasn't fit to kiss Perry Rhodan's boots.

But it just shows the way reputations become inflated. Nostradamus's chief claim to fame is that he got somebody's name wrong! And if you cut Hister out of the predictions — give them a Histerectomy, so to speak — there is *nothing* left, so I content myself with trying to understand what has already happened. Something which is oddly difficult to do...

On to science fiction and fantasy! I can start off by revealing that Harlan Ellison and Gene Wolfe have abandoned their plans to collaborate on a novel. I think they decided that nobody would want to buy a book that had been produced by Harlan & Wolfe.

That concludes my survey of the advances in written SF in the last ten years. I can't say anything about *Battlefield Earth* because I ordered my copy by mail from Ken Slater and it hasn't been delivered yet because Pickford's are on strike. Besides I think it has already been reviewed in *Private Eye* by Richard Ingram.

Another reason for my silence on this subject is that SF writers don't have funny names any more. The names are so *ordinary* these days. You can't make jokes out of them. It's not like in the old days when most of the SF was being produced by people with splendid, resounding names like Stanton A Coblorty and Garrett Putnam Serviss and Delos W Lovelace. One of my favourites was the Russian writer called Nikolai Mikkailovitch Amosov, but he only wrote one novel. He probably figured nobody could become a popular science fiction writer with a name like Amosov. Mind you, I had high hopes of doing a series of puns about the analgesic school of SF writers when Robert Asprin appeared on the scene, but I haven't discovered any other writers whose names sound like cold cures — with the honourable exception of the great Stanislaw Lemsip.

One of the interesting developments in the last ten years has been the upsurge of science fiction and fantasy on the screen. And horror, too. I have to say that I enjoy horror films and occult thriller-type films more than SF films, because the stories seem to translate better onto the screen. It's possibly because the essence of a good science fiction story is an abstract idea, which is naturally difficult to convey as images; whereas the essence of a good horror story is a mood or a feeling, and the cinema is good at evoking moods and feelings. The great advances in special effects techniques must also have something to do with it. Some of my favourite early movies succeeded in *spite* of their special effects, though I seem to remember they were quite good in *Night of the Demon.* Do you remember *Night of the Demon?* That's the movie where Dana Andrews gets a bad attack of the runes. It was quite scary on the large screen, though I think it loses something on video.

That was the other big development of the last decade —

the video revolution. Have you noticed the way nearly everything is a video club these days? I saw loads of signs when I was coming through London: "Funeral Parlour & Video Club"; "Mormon Tabernacle & Video Club"; "Chinese Embassy & Video Club."

One of the things I love about the new wave of glossy movies that began with *Star Wars* is that, *already,* they have developed a brand new set of visual cliches. I still have a fondness for the old cliches that no movie-maker could live without, but they are becoming a bit stale.

For example, how is it that in movieland *everybody* knows what heroin and cocaine taste like? I've seen that bit thousands of times. The story might be set in some sleepy little hamlet in the middle of Dorset. They find the stuff, usually in a plastic bag about the size of a hot water bottle. Nobody stops to reflect that it's worth maybe ten thousand quid. There's always some character who has a huge hunting knife handy, and he whips it out and saws a big hole in the middle of this ten-thousand-pound bag of dope. Then the vicar and the village postmistress grab a handful and cram it into their mouths, and nod, and say, "Yes, that's heroin." How do they *know?*

This astonishing perception on their part is, however, counterbalanced by a strange but universal inability to recognize blood without touching it. I'm happy to say that I very rarely find pools of blood — I never go to the AGMs of the Science Fiction Foundation — but I always know what it is instantly. But in movieland even the most experienced detective *always* dips his finger in it before venturing an opinion.

Then there's the way nobody in a film will ever impart serious news to another person without first ordering him or her to sit down. I think they have to take that precaution because, for some reason, the people who volunteer to break bad news gently are no good at it. If Police Officer Jones gets killed by bank robbers they'll telephone his wife and say, "Hello, is that widow Jones?"

Well, perhaps they're not *that* bad, but after coaxing a nervous and highly-strung woman to sit down they'll stare at her for a few seconds then yell out, "Your mother has just been murdered by a maniac and chopped into little bits and boiled up in a cauldron!"

I mean, they don't even *try* to lead up to the thing in a nice way — though I suppose it would be quite hard to ease your way into a subject like that. It would hardly do to start off by saying, "You remember how your mother always wanted to make good stew...?"

And there's the way when a phone connection gets suddenly broken the person *always* jiggles the rest up and down — which, as everybody knows, only makes the disconnection more final.

The new SF and horror cliches are just as good. The dividing line between the two genres has become a bit blurred with movies like *Alien* and the new version of *The Thing*, which have started a fashion for people suddenly bursting open, and imparted a new meaning to the term "Hurt expression." The movie-makers have also latched on to the shock value of *secretions*. Yugh! I prefer secretions to remain secret. And now there's vomit! Anthony Andrews is building a whole career on his ability to throw up, firstly in *Brideshead*, and then in that post-holocaust play on TV a couple of months ago. I reckon Anthony Andrews has thrown up more times than he has had hot dinners.

But one of my all-time favourite characters in horror was the priest in *The Amityville Horror*. I don't know how he was portrayed in the movie, but in the book he was *great*.

I've become used to the truly heroic type of priest, like the one in *The Exorcist,* who is prepared to die in combat with the Devil — so I was delighted with the priest in Amityville. He was summoned to the house where all the nasty things were supposed to happen, and when he was walking up the front path he *thought* he heard a voice telling him to go away. So he went away!

The book dwells on all the terrifying devilish things that happened to him. When he was driving back home the silencer fell off his car! And even when he was in his own house there were more terrifying manifestations — he got a rash on his hand, and he took a head cold. That sort of thing is enough to break the nerve of even the bravest man, so no matter how many times the owner of the afflicted house phoned and pleaded for him to pop over on his exorcise bike he flatly refused to go. Beautiful!

In science fiction films the new cliches are just as good.

There's usually one major actor who has been brought in because he has no known previous connection with science fiction, which is supposed to lend the whole production stature and respectability. He stumbles through his part looking depressed, baffled and lost — like Forlorn Green — wondering why he has to wear a severe white wig when all the other male actors have beautiful Farrah Fawcett hair styles, or get to dress up in splendid suits of armour made from Austin Seven body panels that have been done up with Zebra grate polish.

And there is always a full complement of those huge rumbling space ships which slowly glide past the camera, looking rather like an aerial view of Barrow-in-Furness. And there's the obligatory daft computer, built out of old Wurlitzer components, which is only there to give an air of authority to stupid decisions. *Star Wars* really set the trend in this respect. The Death Star was designed and run largely by computers, but — following a long-established tradition in space opera — it had a weak spot in its defences. This always takes the form of a little round hole, possibly the overflow from the captain's lavatory, which is just big enough to accommodate a torpedo. On the Death Star it was cleverly positioned at the end of a sort of metallic canyon about a hundred miles long. The canyon was heavily defended by multi-barrelled ray guns all along its length — I think Darth Vader felt he looked good in pompoms — nobody having thought of the more cost-effective idea of putting a metal grille over the little hole.

At the end of the film, when the good guys launched their final attack, somebody in the Death Star's control room said, "The computer has analysed their plan of attack, and it has some merit." We all remember what this meritorious and masterly plan of attack was. It was to enter the hundred-mile canyon — which led to nowhere except that little round hole — at the *wrong* end and fly along it in a straight line, all the while being massacred by pompoms and enemy fighters.

Perhaps I have a naturally devious and sneaky turn of mind, but it seems to me that a better attack plan would have been to tootle around all over the Death Star's surface, pretending you didn't even know about the little round hole, then do a crafty sidestep into the canyon at the *right* end and pop your torpedos into the hole. They managed it in the end, though. I love to think of that torpedo bouncing and rattling along that drain pipe into the bowels of the Death Star, round the S-bends, and finally emerging from the captain's lavatory at a thousand miles an hour — one can only hope the poor guy wasn't sitting on it at the time — then causing that beautiful pyrotechnic explosion... with Harpic and shredded toilet tissue flying all over the place...

For me that is one of the great images of the modern screen, and I think it's an appropriate one with which to end this talk.

BOSH GOES LOCO

The other day I was sitting as is my wont (I always sit this way. I can't help it. Sometimes as I lie taking stock of my life in the long introspective hours of the silent night I say to myself, "BoSh, old chap, you'll just have to stop this sitting as is your wont — give it up while there is still time. Before it gets to be a habit." But it is no use. My wont shakes its head, gives me a smog glance and I have to follow soot. Anything my wont won't want I won't want.) honing the edge of my Ghoodminton bat and thinking to myself that if John Berry could attempt to train a budgie to talk I should be able to train one to hone my bat. Come to think of it, I was just muttering, have I not heard of pigeons that do that? Suddenly Walter spoke to me.

"Do you realise," he said, absentmindedly straightening the barbed wire on the Ghoodminton bat, "that The Glass Bushel is *Hyphen*'s oldest department? The only one in since the beginning!"

I was amazed. Here in Belfast among my circle of inmates I have a reputation for the transient nature of my projects, which usually fade out after a few short days of uncertain existence. Could I have done this glorious thing? After the initial shock had worn off I began to think about my column and all the things that had happened to me since I first began it.

One of the things that immediately springs to mind is the way in which after every GB in which I devoted all my space to a semi-pro-type story, we received an anguished protest from Gregg Calkins, who apparently hates that sort of thing. *Write about fans!* He has said this so often that I am going to do just that to please him. Now. The only fans that I know enough about to enable me to produce an article on them are those here in Ireland and since the arrival of John Berry, sometimes known here as The Chronicleer, this is not possible. He writes up *everything.* I did have the idea of shouting "Copyright" in a loud firm voice immediately anything of interest took place. This worked all right — once. That was the fireworks article a few months back. But John, sensing that his supply of material was being imperilled, only shook his head doggedly, causing a shower — almost Fortean in nature — of old toothbrushes and long lost combs to fly out of his moustache, and retired into the corner to devise his countermove. When he produced his answer to my ploy it was devastatingly simple, as only his sort of brain could produce, and unbeatable.

John now writes up everything *before* it happens. This accounts for the large fantastic element that creeps into his articles and it also means that I have to retract my scope even further. There is only one field of material left.

Me.

From now on every GB will contain some fresh out-pourings, more wordy flows from yet another and another faucet of my character. Now read on...

There is a dark shadow over my life far more ominous

than the one cast by Them in the film of that name, because after all it only took a few army divisions equipped with flamethrowers and bazookas to rout that menace. Nothing to it. But when ordinary, everyday, common or garden insects pick on you, you've had it. There is nothing you can do, you see. When fifteen-foot ants wander about knocking down houses and frightening policemen, the general public is solidly behind you when you start shooting thermite about; *but*, just try anything like that on an ordinary insect and you'll soon find yourself a social outcast.

Why is it necessary to use such drastic measures on poor little creepers, you might say. Well, it all began with the time I brutally murdered two spiders. The first one fell victim to my airgun under very extenuating circumstances which were described in Vin¢ Clarke's late and very lamented *SFN*, so I will not go into that here. The second one I hit with a pickaxe.

I remember the day well. I came out of the drawing office in a hurry to get home to my tea and ran down to the workshop where I had left my bicycle. I was just about to jump on when I noticed a spider, a large stupid-looking spider, dangling around the chain wheel. If I rode away it would get smeared all over everything and I didn't like the idea of that, so I tried to shake it off. It refused to come.

I spent long impatient minutes trying to dislodge the brute and when I finally succeeded I was gibbering with rage. The spider scampered away up the brick wall and it seemed to me that I could detect derision in the way it wobbled its legs. I looked around for something to hit the thing with and my gaze alighted on a huge pickaxe that a workman had left lying about. I hefted it and swung it at the wall grinning ferociously and when I looked to see the result I found an inch-deep hole in the wall with spider's legs sticking out all round the perimeter. They were waving gently like palm trees on the edge of a small lake.

I was immediately sorry for what I had done so I apologised to the tiny crater, looked all about to make sure that I hadn't been seen and rode off home. Another spider must have seen its mate encountering the insect equivalent of the atom bomb though, for, ever since that day, all varieties of tiny winged and many-legged things have been attacking me.

Have you ever been savaged by a moth? I can tell you it is a fearsome sight to see a berserk moth flying at you without a hope of doing you real damage or getting away, like a Jap suicide pilot bent on his own destruction. The night that happened to me I was lying in bed reading when I realised that this moth had entered through the open window.

I decided to treat it with contemptuous disregard and continued to read. Suddenly I felt a stinging blow on the ear and then another on the face as I looked up to see what was happening. At last I realised the horrible truth. I was being attacked by a defenceless moth! Wasps I can handle with ease because I don't mind hitting them and they don't move as fast as a shuttlecock, but this was too much. Mewing with fright I drew back into the corner and made blind swipes at the moth, which was keeping up its insane onslaught. I felt the way Goliath must surely have felt as he noted the fearlessness of David's advance.

Suddenly I landed an uppercut on the moth and then as it was flopping about in the air I sent in a right hook that knocked it into a big box in which I kept books and junk. I went over to have a closer look at the dead hero. I leaned over the box. Boink! It came shooting out again at tremendous speed and hit me on the face.

It was psychological stuff. By this time I was in a dead

funk and it was all I could do to start throwing punches
again, but after a series of panicky swipes I hit the ferocious
moth and as luck would have it, it landed back in the box.
This time I took no chances. I dashed over, almost hysterical
now, and lifted the box and shook it up and down churning
all the stuff inside about like stones in a concrete mixer.
After minutes of this I set the box down and went back to
bed without looking inside.

About half an hour later when I put out the light to go to
sleep I was lying in the darkness when I heard something. It
was the moth fluttering about inside the box among all the
books, old poster colour pots, telescope parts and throwing
knives. I closed my eyes tight and lay there without moving
and, after a long long time, the noise went away.

* * *

The above account is quite true and it shows the horrible
way in which the insects work — they can't win but they fight
anyway. Like the story about the aliens whose way to fight
was to dash up to their enemies and cut their own throats.
Another night I came up to go to bed, threw back the sheets
and was just about to hop in when I realised I had
seen something black disappearing in below the blanket.
Cautiously I pulled the bed clothes back a little further and
discovered a beetle clinging to the sheet.

Now this was a tricky problem. I wasn't going to actually
touch the thing and yet I had to get it off onto the floor so
that it could be disposed of. I dragged the sheet in question
to one side of the bed so that the part to which the beetle was
clinging was hanging over the side and flapped it about with
all my strength. When I had finished the beetle was still
hanging there unperturbed. Feeling the old dread coming

back, I looked around wildly for something to use and I noticed one of those things like mops that are used for polishing linoleum. It was out on the landing. I brought it in, closed the door and played several golfing shots at the beetle. It was no use. In the end I had to put the sheet right down on the floor and sweep the thing off, making a mess of the sheet as I did so. Once on the floor the beetle just sat there, probably picking the torn shreds of linen out of his powerful claws or whatever it is they walk about on. Feverishly I looked about for my shoes; then I remembered I had come upstairs in my socks, so it was the mop again. I put it over the beetle with the handle sticking vertically upwards and leaned on it with all my might, turning it round and round for good measure. When I looked under the mop there was no sign of any intruder so I concluded I had crushed it right into the floor and I set the mop against the wall, changed into my slumber suit and got into bed.

A minute later I saw the beetle come walking out from under the mop. At two in the morning when your confidence in yourself has been badly shaken this is not funny. I leaped out of bed, grabbed the mop and pounded it vertically downwards onto the beetle. In the other bedrooms people began to stir and mutter in their sleep but I was past caring. I looked down and the thing was still there. I began a regular pounding heedless of the startled grunts from the room next door, and after about twelve blows there was no sign of the beetle on the floor.

This time I was not to be fooled. I turned the mop upside down and there it was clinging onto the strands. Giggling faintly I dashed out onto the landing and ran downstairs to the kitchen, determined to burn the beetle to death. The fire had not been lit that day. I set the mop down and the beetle, sensing that I was really out for blood, scuttled out moving at roughly the speed of sound. It went round the room several times looking for a dark place to hide and as our kitchen is small and compact and fairly modern it didn't find one.

When I had overcome the instinctive fear that this unexpected ability to travel like a speeding racer had inspired in me, I lifted one of the heavy chairs so that the front legs were about half-an-inch clear of the floor. It was very dark and safe-looking in below them. The beetle swerved sharply and skidded to a halt under one of the legs.

Feeling ashamed of myself for the underhand trick I had played, I let the chair fall and went up to my bed.

* * *

The above are only two examples taken from my casebook — there are many others. Readers of Paul Enever's *Orion* might remember the description of how a daddy-longlegs drowned itself in my tea, which is another method of attack. However, now that I have got this down on paper I feel better about it all because, if I am ever found dead in an empty room with my eyes glazed over with fear and a water pistol half full of insecticide in my hand, perhaps somebody will remember this and call out a few army divisions equipped with flamethrowers and bazookas and thermite bombs and tanks and rockets to hunt down and destroy the dirty rotten flea or beetle that did it.

* * *

How many fans know that there exists another worldwide organisation which has advantages and interests to offer even greater than those we derive from fandom? The name of this mysterious organisation? It is none other than the Boy Scouts!

Yes, I too have always regarded the familiar Scouts with their proverbial knobbly knees and arrays of badges as being people wasting good energy that could have been used for the production of fanzines. I used to sneer at them and shout "Come on the BB" from the window of the bus when I passed one of their troops, but that is all over now.

The reason for this change of heart? Well, the other night I happened to glance through a copy of *Scouting for Boys* by Lord Baden-Powell, which is the basic literature of the organisation. It is a series of informal lectures, called "Camp Fire Yarns," on the various topics of interest to Scouts. It is the Scout equivalent of *The Enchanted Duplicator*.

In CFY No. 7, which is entitled "Signals & Commands," I came across this interesting little problem. See how you get on with it: it beat me, so I'll give it exactly as in the book to keep everything fair.

> In the American Civil War, Captain Clowry, a scout officer, wanted to give warning to a large force of his own army that the enemy were going to attack it unexpectedly during the night; but he could not get to his friends because there was a flooded river between them which he could not cross, and a storm of rain was going on.
>
> What would you have done if you had been he?

Well, I sat and thought about this for some time and the best I could think of was to get into the river, swim down to the sea, take a boat to India and settle down to planting tea or cotton or something, and find out what happened in the papers. Somehow I was pretty sure this wasn't the right answer so I read on to see what an experienced

scout would have done. Here it is exactly as printed on
p. 56: —

A good idea struck him. He got hold of an old railway
engine that was standing near him. He lit the fire and got
up steam in her, and then started to blow the whistle with
long and short blasts — what is called the Morse Code
alphabet. Soon his friends heard ...

You can just imagine all the Scouts who had been working
on this problem slapping their knobbly knees in self-disgust
and saying, "Of course! Why did I not think of that? It's
the obvious thing to do...." But to me, a member of the
uninitiated, this casual employment of old railway engines
that just happened to be standing about smacked of magic,
another and alien way of thinking.

Puzzled and curious I read on through the book in the
hope of finding something that would throw light on the
problem, then at last I discovered one pregnant sentence that
solved the whole thing. When you knew the real facts there
was actually nothing queer about the idea of a railway engine
and the wherewithal to get up steam in her standing on the
bank of a flooded river during a civil war.

Here is the sentence: —

... but it takes a good deal of practice before a
tenderfoot can get into the habit of really noting
everything and letting nothing escape his eyes.

There was a lot more in the same vein saying that a trained
person can see things that are there all the time but which
the layman cannot perceive through not knowing how. After
thinking this over it dawned on me that there was no mystery
or coincidence at all involved in the episode mentioned. You

see, although we are blind to them and don't know they are there, the whole world is covered with old railway engines and heaps of coal! They are *everywhere.*

When next you go out to work look again at the trolley bus that passes you in the street. Strip away all preconceived notions and attitudes of mind. Now do you not see that it is really a large locomotive? Look at your neighbour's rock garden; is it not really a heap of nutty slack? Those prefabs across the way: is that not something suspiciously like wheels peeping out from below the window box?

Probably most of you, steeped in your habits of thought, will never be able to see through to the real nature of the world around you, and perhaps it is just as well. Just think of the tremendous impact on human affairs if this knowledge became generally accepted! Just considering one aspect of this, the field of literature would be thrown into a state of chaos.

For instance, all those stories of the good girl whose boy friend drops her on a lonely country road in the middle of the night because she refuses to cooperate with him in his nature studies would look pretty silly if you read something like this: —

> What was I to do? I had no idea that Jack would turn out to be the sort of person he was, and as he sat there holding the door of the car open invitingly I was tempted to get back in beside him, for it had begun to rain and I was scared.
>
> My resolution began to waver.
>
> Suddenly I had a good idea. I climbed into an old railway engine that was standing nearby, got up steam in her and drove back to the town. . . .

And furthermore there is no longer any justification for early pioneers in the West making a circle of their waggons and shooting out a losing battle with Indians. The Apaches or Sioux would probably be completely demoralised to see a fleet of old railway engines charging at them from behind a screen of covered waggons. It requires only a little imagination to realise that nearly every great book in the world would be spoiled. Even the titles wouldn't look the same. Who could enjoy a book or a film with such names as:

UNCLE TOM'S DRIVING CABIN
THE ASCENT OF COALHEAP EVEREST
PANDORA & THE FLYING SCOTSMAN
DESIRE UNDER THE L.M.S.

With this disquieting thought planted firmly in your minds I will now conclude this appearance of the Glass Bushel, *Hyphen*'s longest lasting department. If any of you think of any further effects or consequences I would be glad to hear of them so that I can incorporate them into the next GB, thus giving you lots of egoboo and saving me lots of work. In the meantime, I am going to pop over to the loco for a pint.

THE RETURN OF THE
BACKYARD SPACESHIP

I expect you're all wondering why I brought you here tonight... Heh! Heh! Heh!

Well, you must admit this *is* a bit like one of those old movies where an assorted bunch of people find themselves invited to spend a weekend at some really creepy, out-of-the-way spot. I got a couple of mysterious, anonymous notes telling me to come here, and a strange map — just like in the movies. The main difference is that in a film the weekend guests always find themselves in a huge, gloomy, draughty, creaky place, miles from anywhere, with no means of escape. And nobody could say those things about Owens Park. Could they? They're fake fans if they do. But come to think of it... the hall porter does look a bit like Boris Karloff.

This has got me wondering what crimes we all committed in the past. Who did we mortally offend and wants to take revenge on us? Hands up anybody who has ever used *Science Fiction Monthly* to wrap up fish and chips. Hands up anybody who has ever sent a fan letter to *Space: 1999*. I thought so: quite a few of you. That means you'll all start disappearing, one by one. If I'm not mistaken, some people have started vanishing from the back of the hall already! It's funny, but that happened during my last talk, as well...

This talk is going to be about alternative technology, but the subject of *Space: 1999* has cropped up... and in a way, it features alternative technology, too. I mean, the technology in it is *impossible,* and that's a genuine alternative to all this plausible stuff that people like Niven and Asimov and Clarke keep churning out. I missed the first two episodes of *Space:* £19.99p — for some reason, that's how I think of that show — because I pay 10p a week for the *TV Times,* to get extra programme information, and it kept saying that it began at 7.30, whereas it really began at 6.30, and I kept switching on too late. "Just another readers service from Independent Television Publications..." Mind you, it sometimes takes me about an hour to find the programme pages in the *TV Times* anyway, so I might have missed those episodes regardless.

I do know, for example, that in *Space:* £19.99p they are journeying around the galaxy on the Moon, but I never found out what propelled the Moon out of the Solar System. All I know is that it must have been one hell of a powerful explosion, because they reach a different planet every week, and if you grant a high density of stars — say they're about four light years apart — that means the Moon is belting along at 200 times the speed of light! Luckily for Commander Koenig and company, the retro rockets on those Eagle craft seem to be pretty effective — even though they only emit little puffs of smoke, more in keeping with somebody having a crafty drag down in the toilets — and they can always land and chat to the local inhabitants. The residents of these planets all speak English — which is a very lucky thing, too — because I run into language difficulties if I go abroad as far as Italy or Holland or Macclesfield.

Other things I'd like to know about *Space: £19.99p* are: When are they going to show us the vast underground factory which builds the Eagle spacecraft? (A minimum of four of these explode or suffer spontaneous combustion every week, so there *has* to be a big production facility.) When are we going to be told that Barbara Bain is really a robot? Why does everybody in the Moonbase whisper all the time? Why have they got Moon gravity outside the Moonbase and normal gravity inside it? (Maybe *that's* why everybody whispers and looks gloomy — they're introducing extra gravity into the situation.)

Thinking it over, the key to some of these mysteries could lie in something I've already mentioned — the fact that the Moon is travelling at 200 times the speed of light. This means that time in the Moonbase is running backwards, and all the characters in it are heading into their own pasts instead of their futures. Martin Landau is contemplating Missions that are even more Impossible; and Barry Morse is extending the hunt for The Fugitive into interstellar space. "That was no one-armed man, Jansen — that was an inhabitant of Rigel IV waving his proboscis, and you can't touch them for it."

Back to the main subject of the talk — "Lunar Rock: Will It Ever Be As Popular As Martian Country And Western?" No, that can't be right — that's Graham Charnock's talk. Mine is about alternative technology space drives. As you know, space flight is the most common theme in science fiction, and the fact that Moon landings have been accomplished in reality has wiped out whole areas of speculation which many a writer relied upon to earn his living. NASA is taking the bread and butter out of the mouths of science fiction authors, which is not only an immoral thing to do — it's downright unhygienic! Driven out of what used to be their own private territory, SF writers are becoming poorer and poorer. Things have reached the stage at which some of them have to use their Access cards to weigh themselves. Every time I have to take some money out of the bank I feel ill for a couple of hours afterwards — I think it's called a withdrawal symptom.

There is, however, a ray of hope for the future in that present day space technology is not really adequate or suitable for the tasks it has to accomplish, partly because of the fantastic expense involved, and partly because of inherent weaknesses in our whole concept of the space rocket. All the big space powers are looking around for other more efficient, more reliable and more economic ways of getting hardware into the sky, and it is quite possible they will turn to science fiction for fresh, original ideas — for which, I hope, they will pay an appropriate fee. This notion isn't as far-fetched as it might sound, because many leading space technologists have acknowledged the stimulus they get from science fiction. Only the other day I read an article by a big man in the communications satellite business who said he had lost millions of pounds because in 1947 he had thought of, but failed to patent, Arthur C. Clarke. People even come to *me* and ask technical questions. Questions like: "If you put a hole in the middle of a Gemini spacecraft would that make it Apollo?" Or, "Up there in the emptiness of space, what would Isaac Asimov push against?"

Of course, not all the ideas that science fiction has put forward for space ship propulsion are worth following up. A giant gun about a mile high which fires people into space in a bullet is obviously not feasible — partly because of the tremendous accelerations involved, but mainly because you'd never get enough leather to make a holster for it. And it's no good talking about building it underground, with the muzzle at ground level, because it's against the law to have a concealed weapon. You see, it's practical little details like these that trip up some of our most visionary thinkers, but which us hard SF writers have built our reputations on.

A compatriot of mine, who has an equally down-to-earth approach, has pointed out on TV the difficulties that Bell got into when he invented the telephone — it was absolutely no use to him until he had invented another telephone that he could ring up. Then he got carried away and invented a third telephone, and when he rang up the second one it was engaged. That's what's called technological redundancy.

In contrast to some of the quaint old ideas in science fiction, the proposal for a new type of space ship propulsion unit which I'm going to outline to you has all the advantages of being inexpensive and totally practicable. The inspiration came to me one evening when I was sitting at home in an armchair...(have you noticed that chairs are good for sitting on? I keep half a dozen of them round the house for no other reason)...idly toying with a half-pint whisky shandy. My intellect was wrestling with some of the great imponderables of our time, questions like, "Why was the book *The Man Who Folded Himself* written by David Gerrold and not John Creasey?"

Actually, the inspiration came in two parts — just the way Arthur Koestler said it should. That's the way you do creative thinking, by taking two imaginative elements out of your mental stock and synthesising them into something entirely new. I was sitting there watching my television set...(have you noticed that TVs are good for watching? I experimented with watching fridges for a while, and then sideboards, but after this period of trial and error I settled on television sets.)...and a commercial about saving energy came on. It explained, the way they always do, that a big percentage of the heat loss in a house occurs through the windows. That's where your heat goes — right out through the glass of the windows. This information wasn't new to me, but — under the benign influence of the whisky shandies — my intellect was in a highly receptive state, and the stuff about the behaviour of window glass seemed to hang in the forefront of my mind, reverberating in a cryogenic chill. (I copied that last bit out of an *Analog* editorial.)

It's amazing the things which reverberate in the mind after you've had a few drinks — that's why you have such interesting conversations in pubs. The part I like best is when non-SF pub customers start talking about things which we — as science fiction fans, usually with some awareness of science — tend to regard as our own conversational stamping ground. I remember sitting in a little country pub once having a pint with the landlord. Although this was in the Spring, it was a bitterly cold day outside — a fact which seemed to have a depressing effect on mine host. Quite out of the blue, in the middle of a conversation about the price of lettuce, he announced that he had worked out exactly why it was that the weather had become so unseasonal in recent years. My interest perked up at once because I had been speculating about the same thing ever since I saw that *Horizon* programme on BBC which told us that a new Ice Age was going to start the following Tuesday afternoon.

"It's these leap years that's doing it," the landlord explained. "They keep sticking in this extra day every fourth year, and they're all adding up and putting the calendar out of step with the seasons."

Although he didn't realise it, this man was living proof of Weston's Theorem — invented by Pete Weston — which postulates that interest in science fiction usually springs from an underlying appreciation of astronomy. I spent a good thirty minutes with this man trying to make him understand what is actually meant by the terms "year" and "day" and why there's no cosmic linkage between the two, but I simply failed to get through to him. However, this is straying from the point.

The second part of the discovery I was talking about came later on that same evening, when my gaze fell on the second inspirational element, the vital catalyst — which in this case happened to be the inside back cover of the *Radio Times.* You've noticed the way in which certain publications are associated with different types of advertising — the *Daily Telegraph* for jobs; *Penthouse* for saucy French undies; the old *Astounding* for surgical trusses. Not that there's all that much difference between the latter two... between saucy undies and trusses, I mean... in the little illustrations they look equally complicated and disconcerting. Well, the back cover of the *Radio Times* used to be devoted entirely to ads for garages and greenhouses. Nowadays it tends to be given over to glossy adverts for Peter Stuyvesant — the cigarette the tobacconist refuses to sell you unless you produce your passport; and dry Martini — the drink the wine merchant refuses to sell you unless you can produce a licence to fly a seaplane.

At the time I'm speaking of, however, it was still garages and greenhouses, and I got to wondering about the famous Greenhouse Effect. For the benefit of anybody who hasn't read the science column in *Tiger Tim's Weekly,* I should explain that the Greenhouse Effect is a scientific phenomenon, all to do with changing the wavelengths of radiation, by which greenhouse glass refuses to allow heat to pass out through it, thus keeping the greenhouse nice and warm. This was the point at which the two halves of the inspiration began to come together, reaching critical mass.

There's something funny here, I thought, taking a

diminutive sip from my whisky. In an ordinary house the glass in the windows lets all the heat out — but in a greenhouse the glass keeps all the heat *in!*

Suddenly the inspiration was complete.

It dawned on me, there and then, that we could solve all our home heating problems . . . and save the countries of the West billions of pounds in home heating bills . . . simply by taking the ordinary glass out of our windows and replacing it with greenhouse glass!

The idea was so devastatingly simple that for a moment I thought there had to be a flaw in my scientific reasoning. But, no! There was no denying the facts . . . window glass lets heat out, greenhouse glass keeps heat in. Q. E. D. I celebrated my discovery by finishing off the Scotch — reflecting that I could probably afford it now that the Government was likely to vote me an honorarium of a million or two. Then I toddled off to bed, too excited even to bother with my nightly digestive biscuit and cup of Slippery Elm Food.

The big let-down came on the following morning when I was having my usual breakfast of two lightly poached aspirins. There *was* a flaw in my scientific logic, and I cursed myself for not having spotted it immediately. I had done a lot of research into glass while writing my "slow glass" stories, and I knew for a fact that the glass factories did not manufacture two different types — one for ordinary buildings and one for greenhouses. My gleaming inspiration of the previous night had been a tawdry glitter of fool's gold. (That last sentence was a little literary bit I put in as writing practice in case they ever revive *Planet Stories.*) The realisation that I had been wrong lay heavily in me for a while — just like a Brian Burgess meat pie — but then I began to rally as the day wore on. I asked myself, "Would Einstein have given up so easily? Just when things were getting tough, would he have abandoned all his sculptures?"

I think I have pointed out before that it wasn't a huge I. Q. which made Einstein a great scientist; it was his simple and childlike approach — and for all I know, I might be even more simple and childlike than Einstein.

Returning to the problem, I decided that my basic premise about greenhouses had been right, but that I had not been in possession of sufficient facts to construct a viable theory. Some vital clue was missing, but what could it be? (This is just like an episode from *Microbes and Men*, isn't it?) By this time I was hot on the intellectual trail and I consulted my library of science reference works, spending hours going through abstruse works such as *The Penguin Dictionary of Shells; The Shell Dictionary of Penguins; Teach Yourself Embalming; Stand and Deliver — A Treatise on Overcrowding in Maternity Homes; Bionic Men — Would You Let Your Transistor Marry One?; Black Holes — A Successful Treatment Without Surgery*. I even glanced through a manual on dog handling, hoping it might give me a strong lead, but to no avail. This is a weird thing about reference works — I never seem to get anything out of them. I've had a Roget's *Thesaurus* for years, and so far I haven't managed to get a single word out of it. So, it was up to my unaided powers of scientific deduction.

The basic problem was that the manufacturers produced only one grade of glass for normal domestic and commercial use — and yet when sheets of this glass were put into a greenhouse their physical properties mysteriously changed. *Why?* Well, it was Sherlock Holmes who said to Doctor Watson, "When you have eliminated all other possibilities the one which remains, no matter how unlikely, is the best that Conan Doyle could think up on the spur of the moment."

With this truism in mind, I suddenly remembered the reports which have been in science journals lately and which state that vegetables are intelligent. Could it be, I wondered, that vegetables are even smarter than we think they are? Could they be changing the properties of greenhouse glass by mental control, so that they would be kept warm and healthy?

Some of you might think that this idea is a little far-fetched — this notion that vegetables have thoughts and feelings — but is it any more fantastic than some of the things which Einstein asked us to accept in his various theories of relativity? Do you really believe that two men can stand at each end of a moving train, and flash signals to an observer on the bank, without getting thrown off by the ticket collector?

These reports that vegetables have nervous systems and are telepathically aware of their surroundings are perfectly correct, and I can even foresee the day when — perhaps by hormone treatment — we'll be able to give them mobility. There might come a day when vegetables will be accepted as domestic pets, and there's no doubt that in some ways they are more suitable for this role than animals. For example, vegetables like to feed on manure. So you could have this situation in which the average citizen goes out for a stroll in the evening with his pet cabbage on a lead. It would be trotting along behind him — on its little roots — *un*fouling the footpath!

You might even find keen gardeners writing to the newspapers and complaining about how every time they put dung on their roses some thoughtless vegetable-lover allows his pet turnip to stray in and clean the place up. Obviously, there's a whole new field of research here, in deciding which vegetables are the most efficient at modifying glass. I myself suspect the tomatoes, because every time I stare into a greenhouse at them I see them turning a little red.

The more I thought about all this, the more certain I became that I had hit on the only logical answer. Therefore, to save all those billions of pounds on heating bills, all we had to do was put all our glass into greenhouse frames, wait until the tomato plants, etc., inside had altered its trans- mission properties by mental control at the sub-atomic level, then take it away and install it as windows in our houses. Once that was done, all the heat would be kept in, the country would be rescued from the clutches of the oil sheiks, and the national debt would be wiped out in a couple of years.

The only thing which prevented me from immediately phoning the Prime Minister and giving my idea to the nation was the sobering realisation that all the big, powerful combines would seize on it and make even more money than they have now. In particular, the giant glass manufacturers would make vast fortunes overnight and I didn't like the idea of that — mainly because when I was in junior school I was once spat on by a boy called Pilkington. This deeply philosophical consideration decided me to keep my dis- covery to myself, but I give it freely to everybody at this convention.

Some of you — the ones who remember the title of this talk — are saying to yourselves, "What has all this got to do with spaceship propulsion?" Actually, most of you are saying, "What a load of old cobblers!", but *some* of you are saying, "What has all this got to do with spaceship propulsion?" Gerry Webb is, anyway, if he's here.

The answer lies in a straighforward, logical development of the basic idea. To make a really efficient drive unit, all you have to do is take a piece of greenhouse glass and fashion it into a tubular shape and attach it to the back end of your space ship. Up in space the unshielded heat of the sun will pour into this tube and — as we have established that the heat will not be able to escape out through the glass again — the temperature inside will quickly build up and up to a tremendous level. If you feed water into one end of the pipe it will explode into steam and be exhausted through the opposite end at great speed, producing the thrust needed to propel your starship.

Now, if there are any members of the British Interplanetary Society in the audience, they'll no doubt be thinking to themselves that they can see a major objection to the Hot Water Bottle Drive I have just outlined. Those of you who *aren't* technically minded might think it is something to do with the glass of the drive pipes perhaps losing its properties and cooling down. This could indeed lead to a sort of story situation in which Dan Dare is up front piloting the ship when he notices a loss of power and sends the engineer, Scotty, back to investigate. Scotty immediately realises what is happening, so he picks up the intercom and goes, "Oh, Danny boy, the pipes, the pipes are cooling."

But that's comicbook stuff — the real drawback to the Hot Water Bottle Drive which will be troubling all the propulsion engineers in the audience is the old one about reaction mass. They'll be saying you could never carry enough water to give the ship interstellar, or even interplanetary, range. This is a perfectly valid objection — I've read "The Cold Equations" and I know all about this sort of thing — but I'm sure you'll be both pleased and relieved to hear that, through my researches in another scientific field altogether, I've come up with the answer to that one as well.

The inspiration came when I was considering a problem in nutrition. In general, researchers in this field are concerned with lack of nutrition, but in my case the problem seems to be an excess of it. I've checked with other beer-drinkers and they confirm the same thing — every time they have a pint of beer they gain a couple of pounds in weight as well. Now, the really intriguing scientific aspect of all this is that a pint of beer weighs only one-and-a-quarter pounds!

This means that three-quarters of a pound of mass appears from nowhere!

Incredible though it might seem, this process of matter creation within the human body is well authenticated — and it doesn't just happen with booze. Anybody who is a bit fat will tell you that eating just one measly little two-ounce cream bun makes them a pound or two heavier the next day. It's even possible that the entire mass of the universe was created by people eating cream buns and drinking beer, but I'm not interested in cosmology — it's much too airy-fairy and theoretical for me. I prefer to stick to solid, provable facts — such as my discovery about beer.

What, you must be saying to yourselves, does this new discovery of Shaw's do to the Second Law of Thermo-dynamics? Where, you must be wondering, does this extra fluid come from? Well, I don't know where it comes from, but I know where it goes. And this knowledge is the final building block needed for the design of the perfect spaceship.

You start off by installing a small but highly efficient brewery. Next to it goes a well-designed pub with an atmosphere that is conducive to sustained drinking; and beside the pub you, of course, have a toilet. The outlet from the toilet leads into a purifying plant, which receives roughly one-and-a-half pints of liquid for every pint that has been drunk in the bar. Out of every pint-and-a-half of fluid that gets purified, one pint is recirculated back to the brewery — as part of a self-sustaining closed ecology — and the extra half-pint is fed through control valves into a cluster of our greenhouse glass pipes which provide the motive force. Living quarters and a control deck make up the other major compartments.

With this ship you can go anywhere in the Solar System, provided you have a crew of dedicated people who are willing to sit in the bar, for day after day, drinking free beer, with no thought in mind other than getting mankind to the stars. Oddly enough, I think we could round up quite a good space ship crew right here in this hall.

Before you rush away and start building a ship, I should perhaps warn you that life on board won't be all beer and skittles. The beer-drinking complement would be a vital part of the ship, and heavy demands might be made on them occasionally. For instance, if the ship got into a dangerous situation the Captain, up in the control room, would pick up his microphone and say, "Increase speed to Booze Factor Eight," and all the topers down in the bar would have to start drinking twice as fast, whether they wanted to or not. It could be hellish.

Nevertheless, just in case my services are ever called upon to get us to the moons of Jupiter, I think I'll go out to the bar and put in a little practice...

MORE CANADIAN CAPERS

As a film critic in a small way it came as quite a shock to me to learn that I had been under-estimating Hollywood in a rather important point — the blurbs that accompany trailers. The commentators who yammer at top speed during the trailer always seemed to me to have a strange system of logic and ethics which was peculiar to themselves alone. For example, any book which has been lying around for twenty-odd years without being screened is automatically styled "the story that nobody would dare to film before." Another axiom from the chopped-up world of Trailerland is that the proximity of some uncouth geographical feature will inspire like emotions in even the most turgid human breast; burning sands — burning desire: high seas — high courage: naked mountains — naked greed, hatred and so on. Strange as it may seem, *this is quite true,* and in defence of this statement I now present the grim saga of a fan and three nonfans cut off from the world in the cruel, primitive splendour of the Rockies, where nerves are raw, endurance taxed to the limit and where the sound of wheeling vultures is drowned out by the noise of clashing teeth, gears and personalities...dahhh dittadittittitt did ah DAHHHH...

Four men set out on that first overnight expedition of the Pronghorn Hunting Club: Ken Walker (transport), Derek Houghton (artillery), Bob Shaw (beer) and Dave Rhodes (commander). Dave, who has been mentioned in two previous Canadian Chronicles, refuses to go to anything unless he is formally named Commander, a title which he interprets literally and loudly.

The way David saw it was this; we would rendezvous at Ken "The Skel" Walker's house before dawn, he would supervise and coordinate the rest of us loading the Skel's Austin, then he would call out low, terse instructions to the driver and guide the car through the grey, empty streets. The whole business was to be run with the silent grim efficiency of a Commando raid. I don't think we were to be allowed to talk.

The first thing that went wrong was Derek's wife would not let him rendezvous before dawn because he had to help her with the weekend shopping first. This meant that we met at noon under the stares of dozens of curious neighbors who came out in full force to see how we were proposing to carry in one small car, four large men, four piles of blankets, a big tent, four boxes of food, a carboy of water, five rifles, two axes and some miscellaneous effects such as beer, spare clothes, cameras, boots and a voluminous quilt which I had brought along for extra warmth at night. This last item was capable of filling the Austin by itself.

By compressing and rearranging we got everything in all right, except for the people. Dave, who was attired in Army surplus stuff as befitted his rank and was fuming at the lateness of the start and the excited chatter of several Central European types who had stopped to laugh at us, jumped into the front seat and hid behind a Texaco map. Finally Derek and I were tamped into the back seat, where we had to sit on so much equipment that our heads and shoulders were pressed against the roof. The Skel got into the driving seat, started the motor, donned his sunglasses, wedged the forefinger of his left hand behind his upper front teeth and we roared off at about five miles an hour. From my lofty position up at the roof I could not see much outside the car, which was probably why the Skel's peculiar driving position worried me so much.

He had learned to drive only about two weeks before and from what I could see he had not picked it up too well. The engine stalled numerous times in the first mile, we nudged the kerb at corners and narrowly missed several cars and pedestrians. During this whole performance the Skel kept his finger tucked in behind his front teeth and drove with one hand. We guessed later that he was afraid of appearing inexpert in the company of three relatively experienced drivers and that constantly poking an imaginary piece of *filet mignon* out of his teeth was merely the Skel's way of looking nonchalant. It may have made him feel better but the rest of us were terrified. Dave Rhodes had slumped down in the front seat and was not even issuing any commands — a sure sign that he was worried. The little atmosphere that had managed to seep into the car grew tense and the only sound was the wrenching of the gear lever, which the Skel seemed to be trying to remove, and the Skel's violent North of England swearing, which was directed against all other road users in the vicinity.

By the time we reached Cochrane, a small place about twenty miles west of Calgary, the swerving and bouncing of the car had sifted Derek and I down into the equipment somewhat and we could see out. I spotted a hotel and said that we should all go in for a beer. Derek and Dave, both of whom dislike beer, immediately shouted, "Good idea! Let's have a few beers." Grateful to be safely out of the car, we staggered into the hotel and began absorbing draught beer — all except the Skel. He didn't want to impair his driving. He sat around impatiently while we had our drinks and explained all the mistakes all the other drivers he had seen that day were making. When he got tired of that he went out and bought some chocolate for the other members, then there was a row between Dave and Derek about the change they should have received. Convinced that he had been cunningly robbed of five cents, Dave stumped out to the car, the rest followed and we were off on the open road again.

Hours went by bouncing and swerving, cameras kept falling off the back window and hitting me on the nape of the neck, boxes banged against my legs and the huge quilt kept swelling up and up in horrible pink billows which threatened to smother all the occupants of the car. Gradually I was bludgeoned into a sort of beery torpor which was disturbed only by exceptionally vile oaths from the Skel or extra loud moans of panic from David in the front seat.

My fitful repose was finally terminated by the realisation that the Commander had begun commanding rapidly, jumping around in his seat and rattling his sheaf of oil company maps. I peered out and saw that we were rattling along a rutted gravel road in the mountains. We had travelled a little over a hundred miles since noon but the sun was nearing the peaks and greyness was beginning to gather under the trees and in deep clefts in the rock faces. I began to look for a place to camp and set up our base. After ten minutes I saw a little lake away down through the trees and proposed going there.

"No use," barked the Commander, "not enough open

ground. Drive on." Later on I suggested another place and received a similar comment except that this time it was something about the terrain not being suitable for moose. Considering that we were armed with nothing but .22 rifles, except for my Lee Enfield, and had come out with the express purpose of shooting coyotes to have rugs made out of them and that we had no game licences and that it was not the moose hunting season, I felt that the Commander's objection was of a hair-splitting nature. But I kept on spotting nice little places and having them turned down. Then Derek, who was getting tired of bouncing along into the gathering twilight, began seconding my suggestions. Still Dave didn't like them. He had to find the one perfect spot by himself before he would be happy.

At last, when the darkness was almost complete, Dave ordered the Skel to halt. "This is it. H.Q.," he said, pointing out of the car. The place he pointed at was a steep boulder-strewn hillside where the trees grew so thick that you could not see more than a few yards in any direction. The workings of the military-type mind have always amazed me. Every objection that the Commander had made to every place I had proposed could be applied a hundredfold to this dismal place and yet everybody was leaping around with glad cries, unloading equipment, singing and having a good time. I think that the National Service that the English and Scots have to do does serious damage to their minds. In addition to all its other faults this place had one major disadvantage which the rejected spots had not shared — we had just passed a huge notice telling us that we were entering a restricted area and that firearms were forbidden under penalty of fine or imprisonment!

Getting out of the car, I asked David cautiously if he didn't think it was a bad thing not being allowed to use guns if you were on a hunting trip. He brushed me off and began rushing about looking for a spot to erect the tent. Half an hour later the tent was up, the fire was going well and David had erected a little table upon which we were to put all our food so that he could select which stuff he liked best, then he would announce the menu for supper. Dutifully the Skel and I dumped our food onto it along with David's, and David began loading stuff into a huge pan that I had borrowed from my landlady. Suddenly he noticed that Derek, in a flagrant breach of discipline, had whipped out a tiny frying pan of his own and was crouched over the fire cooking sausages in it. Snorting with rage, David ordered him away but Derek, eyes gleaming in the darkness like somebody in *Northwest Passage,* refused to go. David charged the fire with the communal frying pan and a war commenced to see who could take up most of the available flame. The only real loser was the fire, whose every little burgeoning had a frying pan slammed down on it. By the time they had finally beaten the fire out the food had reached a point slightly above body temperature and we ate it, washing it down with instant coffee.

Strangely, it had not become any darker in the past half hour or more. The early twilight had been caused by the proximity of the Kanaskis Range on the west side of us but the upper air had remained bright and everything around us was bathed in a pearly grey light reflected down from the sky. The air was sharp and clean and filled with peace and the millions of pines seemed to be settling down for the night's sleep. The pleasant scene cheered everybody up, the camp was cleared up and a preliminary scouting expedition was made during which Derek, who had disobeyed Dave's orders to remain on guard at the tent and had wandered off, was almost fired at in the mistaken belief that he was a predatory animal sneaking up on the camp. Derek's continued disobedience was getting the Commander down — during their National Service Derek and the Skel had been privates whereas Dave had attained the lofty rank of sergeant and he could not understand why they didn't recognise his authority over them. He sat brooding over this as we gathered around the fire, dug the beer out of the snowdrift where it was stored and settled down for a camp-fire talk.

The camp-fire talk didn't work out too well.

David, who normally takes over on occasions like that, was morose. I had finished my share of the beer and I was watching Derek, who hates beer, to see if he was going to be mean enough to drink all his share simply because he had paid for it. This left it up to the Skel, who was quite satisfied with this arrangement. He described the topography of his home town, all the people in it, their genealogical relationships to each other, his love affairs, his two years in the army which had made him into the mature, sophisticated person he was today, his holiday in Spain and finished up with a little dissertation on bull-fighting which he thought was a grand sport and everybody ought to take it up.

By this time Derek had finished his beer and had turned a luminous green colour. There was some desultory talk during which I watched Derek closely to see what he was going to do. Finally he turned his head round to his left and with a roaring, gurgling sound disgorged beer over everything in that direction. He immediately whipped back round and stared at us with huge, suspicious eyes as if to say, "Who did *that?*" A dead silence descended on the camp — somehow there didn't seem to be anything more to say. The Skel, who had left some stuff in the general area which had been inundated by Derek's were-gargoyle tendencies, got up and poked around gingerly for a few minutes, then disappeared into the tent. We all went in after him and settled down for the night.

For four hours I lay there trying to sleep but there were stones under the tent, I had a pain in my stomach, and the temperature had dropped to not much above zero. None of the others even stirred, they just lay there so quiet and peaceful that I felt like murdering them in their sleep. Finally, when I was about to do a Captain Oates, I heard Dave whisper, "Hey Skel, can you sleep?" After four hours the sound of a human voice came through to me in my agony like the sweet sound of angels. With bated breath I waited to hear if there would be a reply. "No," replied the Skel. "Ah bliddy well can't." I was thrilled — another human voice in my solitude. Then Derek chimed in, "Neither can I." I was delirious with happiness, everybody was awake and had been awake all the time, I had not been alone with my torment. A silence descended inside the tent, then it dawned on me that they were all listening to hear if *I* was awake. In the state of mind I was in this seemed unutterably funny. Clutching my aching stomach I burst into a hideous, cackling torrent of laughter through which I dimly heard people making startled noises and groping for flashlights or weapons. But I couldn't stop laughing. Still whooping like the mad woman in *Jane Eyre,* I got to my feet and staggered out of the tent where I flopped down at the ashes of the fire and began some deep breathing exercises. After a while I calmed down and Dave came crawling out of the tent too.

We made some coffee and had bacon and eggs, which we ate just as the mountain ranges up above us were beginning to glow with the dawn. They seemed to light up from *inside* as though they were made of ice right through and some unknown beings who lived in there were turning their lights on. Leaving the others our bedclothing, Dave and I set out on a hunt which lasted about six hours and during which we saw not one living animal. We got back to the tent about lunch time and had another meal. Not feeling up to more of the type of cuisine available, I contented myself by eating a can of pork and beans cold.

When lunch was over we climbed around a bit and shot a few gophers, but Derek kept disobeying orders — refusing to crawl on his stomach when David told him to and firing at gophers without first pointing them out to David, who had not yet managed to hit anything. So we gave that up and went back to the camp — a decision which was assisted somewhat by the arrival of a Forest Ranger, who told us that because he was in a good mood just this once he wasn't going to confiscate our rifles.

Back at the tent I looked at my watch. One fifteen. If we left at two, even with the Skel driving, we could be in town by six. I could shave and have a hot bath, Sadie would make me a nice supper, then I could sprawl in front of the TV and drink beer all evening. It sounded really nice. I said to Derek I would like to go and he agreed, I said to Dave I would like to go and he agreed too, I looked around for the Skel and saw a weird apparition emerging from the tent. The Skel is six foot three and has no other measurements, and here he was coming out of the dimness of the tent clad in a tiny pair of tight shiny shorts such as muscle men wear in photographs, and carrying (a) a pneumatic mattress, (b) his sunglasses, (c) a bottle of suntan lotion and (d) a thick book. I got a sinking feeling that the Skel, the owner of the car, would not agree to go home.

He didn't.

I could see my pleasant evening fading away to be replaced by one of arriving home at eleven thirty, tired out and dirty, no time for supper, then into bed and before I knew it — up for work on Monday morning. I began to bicker with the Skel but, comfortably stretched out on his mattress and covered with suntan lotion and flies, he ignored everything I said. Presently Derek began to moan at him, and shortly after that the Commander joined in. The Skel bore it all for a while, then he began roaring at us. We roared back. Everybody realised that this was the end of the Pronghorns — the mountains had won!

Presently the Skel had to give in, and in absolute silence we crammed everything back in the car and headed for Calgary. To give him credit the Skel did try to start conversation once. A car appeared in the distance and the Skel said, "Here's a Buick coming," but when we got close it was an Oldsmobile. Nobody said anything to him about it — somehow none of us wanted to talk to any of the others ever again.

UP THE CONJUNCTION

The science talks I've been giving at conventions in the last year or two have — as well as making Isaac Asimov start fretting about the competition — been reprinted in a few magazines. This pleased me no end, except that some letters of comment accused me of occasionally wandering away from the point. I took the criticisms to heart and included in my New Year resolutions a stern directive to myself: Always stick to the point during talks!

It's important to me that I keep this resolution because I had more of them than usual this year, and broke them sooner than usual. You know how it is... you start off the year full of high hopes and lofty ideals... 1978 was the year I was going to save some money, 1978 was the year I was going to get more exercise, 1978 was the year I was going to read *Dhalgren* right through to the end...

They've all gone by the board, except for this one about sticking to the point, so I'm not going to start off with one of my usual preambles about what I was doing at room parties last night. It was just the same old routine, anyway — about two hundred people all crammed together, drinking, smoking, making a hell of a noise, falling down, being sick — and that was just in the lift on the way up!

Actually, when I did get into a party in one of the bedrooms it was so noisy that we got a lot of complaints — from the pilots of Concordes. This afternoon they're going to hold a protest march to stop science fiction fans landing at Heathrow... (They tried phoning the Noise Abatement Society, but the people at the other end of the line couldn't hear them because of the noise.)

Anyway, I mustn't stray away from the subject of this talk, which is about astrology and all its underlying facts and fallacies, and a fascinating new scientific truth I have uncovered about the relationship between human affairs and the movements of the planets. My old sparring partner — the German-Irish writer and researcher, von Donegan — is going to be sick with jealousy when he hears what I've found out. Old Von Donegan (VD, to his friends) is quite peeved with me, you know — over those jokes I made about him in my last talk.

He wrote to me from Germany and threatened to make me into sausage meat, but I wasn't scared. I wrote back and said, "Do your wurst." I thought he would have enjoyed that little bilingual pun, but he told me he had seen it before — on a 20,000-year-old tablet he dug up in Africa.

However, that is beside the point and I promised that all my remarks would be relevant and pertinent. You'll note that I've given the talk a concise clear title — if there's one thing I detest it's this modern propaganda technique of the tricky euphemism which allows unscrupulous people to disguise their motives with fancy words. Like that society that was in the news lately, the one for people who like interfering with small children — Paedophile Information Exchange! It sounds so respectable it could be the governing body of the British Medical Association, or even the British Science Fiction Association.

And there's an even sneakier one on the go now!

The other night I was having a drink in a pub in Bermondsey when I was approached by this shifty-looking character who asked me if I was interested in necrophilia. I said to him, "Do you mean having sex with dead people?"

He looked a bit uneasy at that, glanced all around the place, lowered his voice and said, "Actually, old boy, we prefer to refer to it as posthumous caring."

Horrible and underhanded, isn't it?—but that's the technique they use. I'll bet that if you set up a Society for Posthumous Caring you could get it established as a registered charity and get a member of the royal family as your patron.

Dear me—have I wandered away from the point again? No more of it! Belief in astrology has been with us since ancient times and it is deep-rooted in our thought and language. Men have always had the desire to know what the future held for them, and they have tried many different ways of getting this advance information. They used to, for example, poke around the insides of chickens, inspecting their entrails for signs. Or sometimes they used to sit and inspect the palms of their hands—which is what I'd do if I'd had mine stuck inside a chicken all day. It was a filthy habit, that, though no doubt its practitioners had a great fancy name for it which made it sound respectable. Prediction and Prognostication by Poultry Manipulation, perhaps.

But of all the traditional ways of trying to know the future—cards, divining, consulting oracles, subscribing to the "Racing & Football Outlook"—the stars seemed to offer the best prospects. They were a mysterious and ever-changing spectacle, quite obviously connected with the gods in some way, and it was only logical to assume that they influenced men's destinies. Thus the profession of astrologer sprang up, and it has been with us rather a long time — in spite of the fact that the stars have an infuriating habit of telling us things we don't really want to know, and of presenting the information in language of such peculiar vagueness that any value it might have had is completely dissipated.

Imagine what it must have been like to be an ancient Roman general leading an army which was going to face another army in battle the following morning, a battle whose outcome could shape the future of the world. He goes to his astrologer and asks him for advice about how to run things the next day, and should he throw in his cavalry first and keep the archers till later, and will the barbarians overthrow the empire or will the guttering candle of civilisation be kept alight for another decade. The astrologer does a quick horoscope and gives him the following inside dope, straight from the Horse's Head Nebula: "Personal relationships at the office could be difficult this month, but an old friendship could lead to a new outlook on life. Don't conceal anxieties from your steady boyfriend, and your lucky colour is blue."

That's the sort of thing they always say! Sometimes, in an effort to avoid a general air of vagueness, they particularise a bit by saying things like, "If you were born on a Thursday and have red hair and blue eyes — don't fall out of any tenth-storey windows. The outcome could be distressing." Nobody's going to argue with him on that one, especially anybody who has ever fallen out of a tenth-storey window. Or anybody he landed on. Or sometimes they say, "Wednesday is a day for being careful in business dealings." Of course it is! *Every* day is a day for being careful in business dealings — although, strangely enough, astrologers themselves don't always appreciate that simple truth.

One of my prized memories from my days as a full-time journalist is the one about one of the big Fleet Street publishing empires which, about fifteen years ago, decided to cash in on the general superstitious interest in astrology by starting a new weekly magazine devoted to nothing else but horoscopes and predictions. It was called, I think, *Your Stars* and they got about a dozen of the very best astrologers in the country on the payroll so that they could guarantee to tell all their readers exactly what the future held in store for them.

Unfortunately, the magazine only survived for about a month — because sales didn't come up to expectations! The irony in that is *so* beautiful, and it sums up all my views about astrology.

Astrology as we know it is all a load of bunk.

"That means it isn't a very good subject for a serious scientific talk," you might say. Others might say the whole talk is a bit of a farrago, anyway, and I'm inclined to agree with them because I was born on a Thursday. You know the old rhyme — "Wednesday's child is full of woe; Thursday's child has farrago."

But please note that I qualified my condemnation of the subject by saying astrology *as we know it* is bunk. Other people could have an entirely different approach to astrology, and it is worth remembering that some of the thinkers of old were men of genius. Leonardo da Vinci, for example, was ahead of his time in many ways. I have revealed elsewhere how he created the world's first blue movie. Also, he was famous for his anatomical studies, but not many people know of his connection with early diagnostic medicine...

It came about because he liked working in tempera, which is a type of paint which has eggs as one of its constituents. He also liked working alfresco — he had some funny habits, old Leonardo — and once when he was living on a hill outside Florence he covered the entire outside of his house with a magnificent painting which all the townsfolk used to admire. Unfortunately, the land around his house was infested with a kind of insect which was attracted by the egg in the paint and kept climbing up the wall and eating Leonardo's painting away from the bottom upwards.

He used to counteract this by going out and repainting the picture day by day, but on the days when he wasn't feeling too good he couldn't do that, and the picture used to slowly disappear from the bottom. The townsfolk would look up at his house, shake their heads and say, "Leonardo mustn't be well today — his tempera-chewer is rising." And that's the true origin of that saying.

But that's beside the point... The discoveries I made about astrology came about because I'm an amateur scientist and therefore do not go in for narrow specialisation in one subject. The professional scientist often fails because he channels his mental energy into knowing more and more about one limited subject, whereas I go in for the inter-disciplinary, broad spectrum approach. In fact, it's got to the point where I now know practically nothing about almost everything. In this case, I succeeded because I brought in my experience in the apparently unrelated fields of neurology and optics.

It started a few months ago when I got a bit tired of writing SF and decided to have a break from it. Actually, I was *advised* to have a break from it — by my agent and publisher. Looking back on it, I don't see what my agent got so annoyed about. I had just outlined to him what I thought was a great plot, all about how Winnie the Pooh developed a third eye in the middle of his forehead, a third eye which, naturally, gave him second sight, the way it always does in stories. In the plot he used this extrasensory perception to spy on two meetings of the London SF Circle in the One Tun. My agent seemed a bit uncertain about the commercial value of the proposed story, and he seemed to blow his top altogether when he heard I was going to call it "One Tun, One Tun, Middle Eye Pooh."

Anyway, the upshot was that I turned my restless inquiring mind to other activities for a while. I didn't delve into astrology immediately, or even neurology or optics, because I had got involved with the mystery surrounding the legend of the Flying Dutchman. I have always felt sorry for that poor bloke, condemned to sail around the oceans and seas of the world forever, never able to take a minute's rest, like somebody working his way through college by selling subscriptions to *Science Fiction Monthly*.

Eventually I proved to my own satisfaction that he wasn't haunted or anything like that — he had simply lost control of his ship. The culprit was a wood-boring parasite (related to da Vinci's insects) which originated in Holland and which had a special liking for the hardwood used in the steering wheels of all ships built in Holland. It used to eat them away, leaving the captain with no means of steering. You may have heard the name I gave it — Dutch helm disease.

Having disposed of yet another famous mystery, I was looking around for something else to do when Joe, the owner of a local lawn mower factory up in Ulverston, telephoned and asked me to have lunch with him to discuss a problem. He sounded as though it was pretty urgent, which surprised me because one of the things I like about Ulverston is that nothing ever happens there in a hurry. The town's chief claim to fame is that Stan Laurel was born there. When I first went to Ulverston I used to think it was quite remarkable that Stan Laurel should have been born there, out of all the places in the world — then when I got to know the place I realised he couldn't have been born anywhere else. It's a sleepy Stan Laurel sort of a town, where there's never any rush about anything. In fact, I said to one of the men in the local pub, "The philosophy around here seems to be mañana." He said, "What does mañana mean?" I said, "You know — it'll do tomorrow." And he said, "Oh, there's nothing as urgent as that around here."

But Joe was obviously in a hurry, so I arranged to meet him that day, quite pleased at the prospect of a slap-up business lunch. My wife didn't seem too pleased, though. She warned me that I had a habit on occasions like that of eating and drinking far too much.

"It's all right," I quipped, "I'll put it on my Excess card." (She believes in moderation, but I think moderation is only all right in moderation. Excess is better, provided you don't have too much of it.)

I then went out and jumped into my new car. I have to jump into it — there aren't any doors. That's because it's a souped-up job — a Morris Oxtail. The thing I like most about it is that it has a very reliable Italian engine whose manufacturers didn't put it into production until no less than two thousand Italian engineers had checked the design and given their approval and consent. That means, of course, that it is a two thousand *si-si* engine.

All that aside, I went and met Joe for lunch and, to give him his due, I must say he really lashed out. He missed me though. Actually, it was a pub lunch and he bought me a Cumbrian pheasant, which is a sausage with a feather stuck in it. I had been recommended to him by a mutual friend, a fellow journalist who is the science correspondent for the *Beano*, but he seemed a bit doubtful about my qualifications, especially my connections with science fiction.

"Science fiction," he said, "isn't that those magazines with covers showing girls dressed in nothing but little bits of brass?"

"Yes," I leered, "but just think of the new dimension that gives to the hobby of brass rubbing."

That seemed to reassure him, because he was a really lecherous looking character — the sort of person who could think impure thoughts about Margaret Thatcher. He said, "Doesn't James White write science fiction?"

"Yes, but not only science fiction," I told him. "He's now working on an Irish political musical called 'Don't Cry For Me, Ballymena.' It's a follow-up to his successful nude review, 'Oh, Balbriggan.'"

That seemed to allay all his fears, so he told me about his problem, which was that his firm had built a new office block, but when the staff had moved into it their productivity had fallen away to almost zero.

"They don't seem to think properly any more," he said. "The only time they seem to get any good ideas is when they're in the lavatory."

It was obvious from the look on his face that he thought the problem was insoluble, and when I asked him to sketch a typical layout for one of his offices he complied without much enthusiasm, and did a drawing like Diagram A.

"Aha, I *thought* so," I said triumphantly. You should have seen his little face light up — he looked like a NASA official being told that the Mars landers had dug up definite proof of the existence of Ray Bradbury.

"Do you mean," he said, with a hopeful tremor in his voice, "you know what's wrong?"

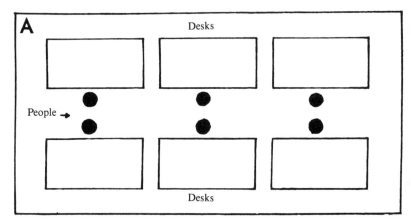

"Of course," I said. "It's a clear-cut case of encephalic field interference."

It may have been my imagination, but it seemed to me that the look of joy on his face died out of his face a little when I said that. I went on and explained to him that the active human brain is surrounded by a faint electro-magnetic field which extends several feet beyond the skull. (The only known exception to this is in the case of fans of the TV show *Space: 1999*. Their skulls are too thick to allow anything to pass through.)

When people are crammed too close together their brain fields interfere with each other and that causes a severe damping down of the powers of thought — as you will be able to prove for yourself if you go to any of the room parties tonight. I explained to Joe that all he had to do was move his staff round to the other side of their desks, thus separating them enough to allow their brain fields full play, without any unwanted reflection from walls either, and everything would be all right.

"This is marvellous," he said, finally convinced. "The firm has lost so much money lately that I can't pay you in cash, but if you like I'll give you a lawn mower out of my factory."

I said, "No mower for me thanks — I'm driving."

We parted and I returned to my study to embark on some more vital scientific research. On the face of it, it appeared that I had wound up yet another successful case — and yet something was troubling me. I had a feeling that I had been on the verge of a major scientific discovery, that something that had been said during our meeting had contained a small and apparently insignificant clue to something else, a clue that I had missed. And as anybody who watches *Horizon* and similar TV shows will tell you, small and apparently insignificant clues are the very best sorts for scientific researchers. Big significant clues are a complete waste of time — but when you get a small and apparently insignificant clue you know you're really on to something good.

With the small voice clamouring at the back of my mind, I got down to work on another project of mine — the design for a spaceship engine powered by the heat from continental quilts. Continental quilts, or duvets, are marvellous things, you know — even though they're so expensive. When I was a kid, and this shows how times have changed, every bed in every house in the country, even the poorest, had a duvet on it — only we didn't know they were duvets. We called them eiderdowns.

And because we didn't know how they worked — there were no Sunday colour supplements to explain it all to us — we used them wrongly. In the wintertime we put a sheet on the bed, followed by twenty woollen blankets, and put the duvet, or eiderdown, on top of all that — and we still froze every night. What was happening, you see, was that the duvet was heating the top ten layers of blankets, but that heat couldn't filter all the way down to us.

I worked on the spaceship engine for a while, but my mind wasn't able to grapple properly with the problem. I put it aside and dabbled a little with a paper I was writing on criminology which puts forward the theory that, just as some people claim that sex education in schools can lead to juvenile rape, the teaching of economics can incite schoolboys to go out and rob banks. But my heart wasn't in that project either, so I picked up a book on the science of optics and was idly glancing through it when, by purest chance, my gaze fell on a paragraph about Fresnel lenses. There was a diagram there showing what a Fresnel lens was like, and as I looked at it I felt something strange and powerful begin to well up inside me. It was the sausage I had eaten in the pub at lunchtime. A couple of indigestion tablets calmed my stomach down a bit, and I began studying the diagram again with the beginnings of a heady intellectual excitement. I knew I was on the verge of a breakthrough. (So was the sausage, but I was too busy to care.)

An ordinary lens has a single continuous curve, which means that a big lens tends to be very thick and heavy, which is a drawback for most applications. A Fresnel lens follows the same curvature, but keeps stepping down at close intervals so that you get roughly the same focussing effect with far less volume of glass or plastic.

I stared at the cross-section of the Fresnel lens — with

half-formed ideas heaving in my subconscious — and tried to identify what it reminded me of, something from another field of knowledge altogether. Suddenly I had it! It was all there in front of me! No, not the sausage — I don't believe in flogging a joke to death — but the answer to the questions that had been niggling me all afternoon.

The Fresnel lens resembled nothing more than a cross-section through an ancient Roman amphitheatre!

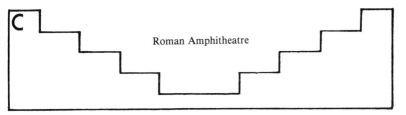

Roman Amphitheatre

Like a man in a hypnotic trance, I heard Joe's voice once again saying, "The only time they seem to get any good ideas is when they're in the lavatory." *That* was the small and apparently insignificant clue I had missed. People *do* tend to think well when they are in the toilet, but according to my theories of encephalic field interference that should have been impossible because of the notorious smallness of office toilets. It dawned on me that I had made the mistake of thinking like a Flatlander — only considering the brain field in the two-dimensional terms of a plane. And the solution to this sub-problem lay in the fact that office toilets, although small in floor area, are usually high-ceiling affairs — and that allows the brain fields to extend upwards without hindrance. I had been making the mistake of forgetting all about the third dimension.

What has all this to do with Fresnel lenses, Roman amphitheatres, and astrology?

Well, just imagine thousands and thousands of people packed onto the terraces of the amphitheatre. It's just like a lens — or, more correctly, a mirror — focussing all their brain fields upwards into a psychic beam of unimaginable power. A concentrated torrent of human mind force which is being shot into space like an invisible searchlight beam!

The mind-shaking question was: What effect would such a beam have on any distant planet it happened to strike?

With trembling fingers I got out the calculator I had borrowed from Robert Silverberg — it's the one he uses to calculate how many novels he can write in a week — and did a few sums. A minute of high-speed computation showed me that at 3.15 on the afternoon of July 2nd in the year 80 AD...just as the newly-completed Colosseum in Rome was being used for its first gladiatorial combats...with the terraces filled with 100,000 blood-crazed spectators...the planet Mars was precisely at zenith.

We may never know what Mars looked like before that fateful moment.

It may have been a green and pleasant world...a place of tinkling streams and peaceful meadows, where colourful birds chattered among the gently nodding trees — but in an instant it was transformed, by the ravening force of all those minds filled with images of blood-stained sand, into the Mars we know today. The planet of endless red deserts.

Venus got the treatment next. It strayed into the beam from the big amphitheatre in Tunisia, but it was during the interval and there was nothing going on in the arena — so it just got turned into a ball of hot white sand.

Jupiter was unlucky enough to be caught in the beam emanating from one of the very earliest Welsh poetry and song competitions, held in a natural amphitheatre in Glamorgan, and it got turned into a huge ball of hot gas.

My researches haven't yet revealed what happened to the other planets in the Solar System, but at least now we know that there is a direct link between human beings and the planets and stars. The only trouble is that the astrologers, not being coldly logical thinkers like me, have got everything backwards. Astrologers on distant worlds must be important people because they can warn their customers about *Earth* being in the ascendancy. When they talk about Earth being in the seventh house, you'd better sit up and pay attention. We influence the heavenly bodies — and what a dreadful responsibility it is. Just think what the audience at a Linda Lovelace film could do to an unsuspecting little planet like Mercury. It hardly bears thinking about.

The only bright spot I can find in all this is that in August next year when the Worldcon is being held the Moon will be high in the sky above Brighton. If the convention hall is the right shape, and if we all work very hard at it and think the right kind of thoughts, we might be able to turn the Moon into a permanent science fiction convention. It seems to me that that's the sort of noble, yet practical, common cause which is just what the science fiction community needs to prove to the rest of the world that we aren't merely impractical visionaries.

See you up there!